THE CASE OF THE
CHICAGO FAMILY WAR

Volume 8: Zen and the Art of Investigation

ANTHONY WOLFF

authorHOUSE®

AuthorHouse™
1663 Liberty Drive
Bloomington, IN 47403
www.authorhouse.com
Phone: 1-800-839-8640

Published by AuthorHouse 05/15/2014

ISBN: 978-1-4969-0154-5 (sc)
ISBN: 978-1-4969-0150-7 (e)

Dedicated to Architect Laura W. R.

PREFACE

WHO ARE THESE DETECTIVES ANYWAY?

"The eye cannot see itself" an old Zen adage informs us. The Private I's in these case files count on the truth of that statement. People may be self-concerned, but they are rarely self-aware.

In courts of law, guilt or innocence often depends upon its presentation. Juries do not - indeed, they may not - investigate any evidence in order to test its veracity. No, they are obliged to evaluate only what they are shown. Private Investigators, on the other hand, are obliged to look beneath surfaces and to prove to their satisfaction - not the court's - whether or not what appears to be true is actually true. The Private I must have a penetrating eye.

Intuition is a spiritual gift and this, no doubt, is why *Wagner & Tilson, Private Investigators* does its work so well.

At first glance the little group of P.I.s who solve these often baffling cases seem different from what we (having become familiar with video Dicks) consider "sleuths." They have no oddball sidekicks. They are not alcoholics. They get along well with cops.

George Wagner is the only one who was trained for the job. He obtained a degree in criminology from Temple University in Philadelphia and did exemplary work as a investigator with the Philadelphia Police. These were his golden years. He skied; he danced; he played tennis; he had a Porsche, a Labrador retriever, and a small sailboat. He got married and had a wife, two toddlers, and a house. He was handsome and well built, and he had great hair.

And then one night, in 1999, he and his partner walked into an ambush. His partner was killed and George was shot in the left knee and in his right shoulder's brachial plexus. The pain resulting from his injuries and the twenty-two surgeries he endured throughout the year that followed, left him addicted to a nearly constant morphine drip. By the time he was admitted to a rehab center in Southern California for treatment of his morphine addiction and for physical therapy, he had lost everything previously mentioned except his house, his handsome face, and his great hair.

His wife, tired of visiting a semi-conscious man, divorced him and married a man who had more than enough money to make child support payments unnecessary and, since he was the jealous type, undesirable. They moved far away, and despite the calls George placed and the money and gifts he sent, they soon tended to regard him as non-existent. His wife did have an orchid collection which she boarded with a plant nursery, paying for the plants' care until he was able to accept them. He gave his brother his car, his tennis racquets, his skis, and his sailboat.

At the age of thirty-four he was officially disabled, his right arm and hand had begun to wither slightly from limited use, a frequent result of a severe injury to that nerve center. His knee, too, was troublesome. He could not hold it in a bent position for an extended period of time; and when the weather was bad or he had been standing for too long, he limped a little.

George gave considerable thought to the "disease" of romantic love and decided that he had acquired an immunity to it. He would never again be vulnerable to its delirium. He did not realize that the gods of love regard such pronouncements as hubris of the worst kind and, as such, never allow it to go unpunished. George learned this lesson while working on the case, *The Monja Blanca*. A sweet girl, half his age and nearly half his weight, would fell him, as he put it, "as young David slew the big dumb Goliath." He understood that while he had no future with her, his future would be filled with her for as long as he had a mind that could think. She had been the victim of the most vicious swindlers he had ever encountered. They had successfully fled the country, but not the range of George's determination to apprehend them. These were master criminals, four of them, and he secretly vowed that he would make them fall, one by one. This was a serious quest. There was nothing quixotic about George Roberts Wagner.

While he was in the hospital receiving treatment for those fateful gunshot wounds, he met Beryl Tilson.

Beryl, a widow whose son Jack was then eleven years old, was working her way through college as a nurse's aid when she tended George. She had met him previously when he delivered a lecture on the curious differences between aggravated assault and attempted murder, a not uninteresting topic. During the year she tended him, they became friendly enough for him to communicate with her during the year he was in rehab. When he returned to Philadelphia, she picked him up at the airport, drove him home - to a house he had not been inside for two years - and helped him to get settled into a routine with the house and the botanical spoils of his divorce.

After receiving her degree in the Liberal Arts, Beryl tried to find a job with hours that would permit her to be home when her son came home from school each day. Her quest was daunting. Not only was a degree in Liberal Arts regarded as a 'negative' when considering an applicant's qualifications, (the choice of study having demonstrated a lack of foresight for eventual entry into the commercial job market) but by stipulating that she needed to be home no later than 3:30 p.m. each day, she further discouraged personnel managers from putting out their company's welcome mat. The supply of available jobs was somewhat limited.

Beryl, a Zen Buddhist and karate practitioner, was still doing part-time work when George proposed that they open a private investigation agency. Originally he had thought she would function as a "girl friday" office manager; but when he witnessed her abilities in the martial arts, which, at that time, far exceeded his, he agreed that she should function as a 50-50 partner in the agency, and he helped her through the licensing procedure. She quickly became an excellent marksman on the gun range. As a Christmas gift he gave her a Beretta to use alternately with her Colt semi-automatic.

The Zen temple she attended was located on Germantown Avenue in a two storey, store-front row of small businesses. Wagner & Tilson, Private Investigators needed a home. Beryl noticed that a building in the same row was advertised for sale. She told George who liked it, bought it, and let Beryl and her son move into the second floor as their residence. Problem solved.

While George considered himself a man's man, Beryl did not see herself as a woman's woman. She had no female friends her own age. None. Acquaintances, yes. She enjoyed warm relationships with a few older women. But Beryl, it surprised her to realize, was a man's woman. She liked men, their freedom to move, to create, to discover, and that inexplicable wildness that came with their physical presence and strength. All of her senses found them agreeable; but she had no desire to domesticate one. Going to sleep with one was nice. But waking up with one of them in her bed? No. No. No. Dawn had an alchemical effect on her sensibilities. "Colors seen by candlelight do not look the same by day," said Elizabeth Barrett Browning, to which Beryl replied, "Amen."

She would find no occasion to alter her orisons until, in the course of solving a missing person's case that involved sexual slavery in a South American rainforest, a case called *Skyspirit*, she met the Surinamese Southern District's chief criminal investigator. Dawn became conducive to romance. But, as we all know, the odds are always against the success of long distance love affairs. To be stuck in one continent and love a man who is stuck in another holds as much promise for high romance as falling in love with Dorian Gray. In her professional life, she was tough but fair. In matters of lethality, she preferred *dim mak* points to bullets, the latter being awfully messy.

Perhaps the most unusual of the three detectives is Sensei Percy Wong. The reader may find it useful to know a bit more about his background.

Sensei, Beryl's karate master, left his dojo to go to Taiwan to become a fully ordained Zen Buddhist priest in the Ummon or Yun Men lineage in which he was given the Dharma name Shi Yao Feng. After studying advanced martial arts in both Taiwan and China, he returned to the U.S.

to teach karate again and to open a small Zen Buddhist temple - the temple that was down the street from the office *Wagner & Tilson* would eventually open.

Sensei was quickly considered a great martial arts' master not because, as he explains, "I am good at karate, but because I am better at advertising it." He was of Chinese descent and had been ordained in China, and since China's Chan Buddhism and Gung Fu stand in polite rivalry to Japan's Zen Buddhism and Karate, it was most peculiar to find a priest in China's Yun Men lineage who followed the Japanese Zen liturgy and the martial arts discipline of Karate.

It was only natural that Sensei Percy Wong's Japanese associates proclaimed that his preferences were based on merit, and in fairness to them, he did not care to disabuse them of this notion. In truth, it was Sensei's childhood rebellion against his tyrannical faux-Confucian father that caused him to gravitate to the Japanese forms. Though both of his parents had emigrated from China, his father decried western civilization even as he grew rich exploiting its freedoms and commercial opportunities. With draconian finesse he imposed upon his family the cultural values of the country from which he had fled for his life. He seriously believed that while the rest of the world's population might have come out of Africa, Chinese men came out of heaven. He did not know or care where Chinese women originated so long as they kept their proper place as slaves.

His mother, however, marveled at American diversity and refused to speak Chinese to her children, believing, as she did, in the old fashioned idea that it is wise to speak the language of the country in which one claims citizenship.

At every turn the dear lady outsmarted her obsessively sinophilic husband. Forced to serve rice at every meal along with other mysterious creatures obtained in Cantonese Chinatown, she purchased two Shar Peis that, being from Macau, were given free rein of the dining room. These dogs, despite their pre-Qin dynasty lineage, lacked a discerning palate and proved to be gluttons for bowls of fluffy white stuff. When her husband retreated to his rooms, she served omelettes and Cheerios, milk instead of tea, and at dinner, when he was not there at all, spaghetti instead of chow mein. The family home was crammed with gaudy enameled furniture and torturously carved teak; but on top of the lion-head-ball-claw-legged coffee table, she always placed a book which illustrated the elegant simplicity of such furniture designers as Marcel Breuer; Eileen Gray; Charles Eames; and American Shakers. Sensei adored her; and loved to hear her relate how, when his father ordered her to give their firstborn son a Chinese name; she secretly asked the clerk to record indelibly the name "Percy" which she mistakenly thought was a very American name. To Sensei, if she had named him Abraham Lincoln Wong, she could not have given him a more Yankee handle.

Preferring the cuisines of Italy and Mexico, Sensei avoided Chinese food and prided himself on not knowing a word of Chinese. He balanced this ignorance by an inability to understand Japanese and, because of its inaccessibility, he did not eat Japanese food.

The Man of Zen who practices Karate obviously is the adventurous type; and Sensei, staying true to type, enjoyed participating in Beryl's and George's investigations. It required little time for him to become a one-third partner of the team. He called himself, "the ampersand in *Wagner & Tilson.*"

Sensei Wong may have been better at advertising karate than at performing it, but this merely says that he was a superb huckster for the discipline. In college he had studied civil engineering; but he also was on the fencing team and he regularly practiced gymnastics. He had learned yoga and ancient forms of meditation from his mother. He attained Zen's vaunted transcendental states which he could access 'on the mat.' It was not surprising that when he began to learn karate he was already half-accomplished. After he won a few minor championships he attracted the attention of several martial arts publications that found his "unprecedented" switchings newsworthy. They imparted to him a "great master" cachet, and perpetuated it to the delight of dojo owners and martial arts shopkeepers. He did win many championships and, through unpaid endorsements and political propaganda, inspired the sale of Japanese weapons, including nunchaku and shuriken which he did not actually use.

Although his Order was strongly given to celibacy, enough wiggle room remained for the priest who found it expedient to marry or dally. Yet, having reached his mid-forties unattached, he regarded it as 'unlikely' that he would ever be romantically welded to a female, and as 'impossible' that he would be bonded to a citizen and custom's agent of the People's Republic of China - whose Gung Fu abilities challenged him and who would strike terror in his heart especially when she wore Manolo Blahnik red spike heels. Such combat, he insisted, was patently unfair, but he prayed that Providence would not level the playing field. He met his femme fatale while working on *A Case of Virga*.

Later in their association Sensei would take under his spiritual wing a young Thai monk who had a degree in computer science and a flair for acting. Akara Chatree, to whom Sensei's master in Taiwan would give the name Shi Yao Xin, loved Shakespeare; but his father - who came from one of Thailand's many noble families - regarded his son's desire to become an actor as we would regard our son's desire to become a hit man. Akara's brothers were all businessmen and professionals; and as the old patriarch lay dying, he exacted a promise from his tall 'matinee-idol' son that he would never tread upon the flooring of a stage. The old man had asked for nothing else, and since he bequeathed a rather large sum of money to his young son, Akara had to content himself with critiquing the performances of actors who were less filially constrained than he. As far as romance is concerned, he had not thought too much about it until he worked on *A Case of Industrial Espionage*. That case took him to Bermuda, and what can a young hero do when he is captivated by a pretty girl who can recite Portia's lines with crystalline insight while lying beside him on a white beach near a blue ocean?

But his story will keep...

TUESDAY, JANUARY 3, 2012

The voice mail message from Martin Mazzavini had been left on Beryl's phone at 4 a.m. This meant that it was 3 a.m. in Chicago when he made the call. Why would he be calling in the middle of the night?

It was morning when Beryl returned the call.

Martin Mazzavini had been sitting in his grandfather's hospital room all night, watching the old man breathe with the aid of a ventilator. He had set his phone to vibrate, and when Beryl's call came in, he was groggy, stiff, and slow to respond. In the time it took him to collect himself and answer, Beryl was recording a message to him. He interrupted her, whispering, "Can you come out here. I need you badly."

"What's the problem?"

Martin went out into the hall. "I'm at Chicago Memorial. My grandfather was hurt bad last Sunday - New Year's Day. The doctors say he'll be ok. But this is the fourth so-called accident he's had in the last month. I wasn't going to bother you, but I had nightmares last night sitting in the chair here. He had a couple of bruised ribs and was having trouble breathing, so they put him on a ventilator. They're gonna remove it this morning. I'm goin' nuts trying to figure this out."

"What happened?"

"That's what I want to hire you to find out. Somebody tried to run him off the road. This Saturday night he'll be having his 75th birthday party. The doc says he'll be out of here in a couple of days and that he can go to his party. I'd like you to come, too. And before the party begins, I'm hoping you can find out what the hell is goin' on here. Can you come?"

"Yes, of course. I'll make a few arrangements. George can cover for me. When do you want me to arrive?"

1

"Can you be here for lunch?" he laughed.

At O'Hare Airport, Martin Mazzavini, wearing a fresh Armani suit which replaced the one that had been much abused during a night spent sleeping in a hard hospital chair, stood at the gate and watched the passengers emerge from the jetway. It had been half a year since he had seen Beryl Tilson. "She will by flying coach," he told himself, "and be among the last to deplane. It's that Zen thing."

Mazzavini, exceedingly handsome and fashionably attired "for success," succeeded in looking either like an up-and-coming young lawyer or an impeccably dressed aspiring mafioso. It was difficult to decide which. More than his attire and cologne inspired curiosity to those around him as he waited. Who, they wondered, would he be greeting?

Beryl disappointed them. The rush to get to Chicago caused her to cut a few corners in preparation. Her hair was stringy, she wore no make-up, her jeans were faded, her sneakers battered, and, since her good jacket was in the cleaners, the jacket she wore camping - a bright orange creation - looked more than a little odd. As if she were trying to dodge an extra charge for luggage, she came down the jetway carrying a purse, a large tote bag, and a rolling carry-on suitcase. She was also fifteen years older than the finely tailored man who waited for her. People looked away. She had cost him their interest.

Martin hugged her as he took the suitcase in hand. "Thanks for coming. Anything in baggage?"

"No. I thought you'd be anxious to get moving. For what I need, I can always buy clothing in a supermarket. I brought my cowboy boots. Will I need 'em?"

"I hope so. Did you bring a party dress?"

"Yes. Sensei bought it for me in Suriname."

Martin tugged at his tie's knot and decided against inquiring further. "I'm not even gonna' ask. I'll take you if you're wearing a sarong or a grass skirt."

"Boy! Is that a load off my mind."

Martin Mazzavini liked to be teased by Beryl. The joking established a reassuring familiarity that allowed him to speak confidentially. "You know how crazy I am about my grandfather. Somebody's out to get him."

"Your 'Pop Pop' is the last man I'd figure who'd be a target for a fatal accident. How is he?"

"He's breathing on his own and sitting up. I'll bring him home day after tomorrow."

"Did you post guards at his door?"

"Yes. Around the clock. He's mad as hell. Says it's a waste of time and money. My father is getting him a bodyguard. Ok. Where do you want to stay? If you want to stay downtown, I'll take you to a hotel... any one you want. If you want to stay at the country club where we're giving my grandfather the birthday party, you can stay there. We have a permanent suite at the club. It's just two rooms. Or you can stay with me."

"What kind of accommodations do you have?"

"Two bedrooms."

"What do you use the other one for?"

"Don't worry. I don't have anything in there that moves."

"Still haven't got the hang of it?"

Mazzavini laughed. "They move. For me they move. I pay them extra."

"You're a lawyer. Threaten them with a non-performance lawsuit."

He put his arm around her neck and pulled her off-balance as they walked. Mazzavini laughed. "You can't imagine how much I've missed you. I live in a world of phonies. Phony innocents. Phony rich. Phony lovers. Phony friends." He sighed, "And the most real guy, the greatest guy in the world, is being hurt by some lunatic... and Jesus, Beryl, I don't know how to protect him." He took her elbow and guided her onto the moving walkway. "Ah, I'll explain it all when we get home."

Beryl made tea as Martin checked with the hospital. "He's asleep and all's well."

3

"Tell me all you know. First tell me the facts and then we'll discuss your interpretation of the facts. But don't mix them up." Beryl got out a little blue notebook and began to take notes.

"This has to do with a family who owns and operates Calvino Investments," Martin began, "which was founded before World War I, by Antonio Calvino, from the old country. My grandfather has represented them since 1971.

"Antonio Calvino, the founder, had three sons who all worked for him: Giovanni, who was a friend of my grandfather's since they were kids; Lorenzo; and Paolo. They were all born in the thirties so I can give you only my grandfather's opinion of them. Giovanni was a nice guy - honest and hardworking. Lorenzo thinks he's clever, but he's just slick - if you can appreciate the difference - sleazy and cutthroat. You'll be meeting him, his wife, and his five kids - four of whom are absolutely worthless. And the third son was Paolo, the youngest and the family black sheep. He was an esthete, and an anti-war activist. My grandfather says he was a 'hippy flower child.' I'm not entirely sure of what that is, but he wanted to become a poet or songwriter. Antonio would not permit a son of his to write poetry, so Paolo entered college on track for a business degree like his brothers Lorenzo and Giovanni." He waited until Beryl finished jotting down information in her little blue tablet. "Do you have all that?" he asked.

"Antonio Calvino, founder of Calvino Investments. Three sons: Lorenzo - and you used the past tense for Giovanni and Paolo. Are they dead?"

"Yeah. Only Lorenzo's alive and he's a major part of the problem. So here's the backstory. When Paolo was in his freshman year in college, he got a girl named Lucille pregnant and he married her. The Calvino family went through the usual stages of rage: she wasn't Catholic, she wasn't Italian, she wasn't a virgin; and she wasn't rich. An Italian Catholic axe murderess would have been acceptable... if she were a virgin. Lucille did not qualify. You'd have to be Italian to understand. Paolo had committed a crime against the family and they weren't about to become accessories after the fact. Paolo was cut loose.

"Paolo left school and got a job, but then Antonio relented and gave him a low-level job in the Calvino Investment Company. Antonio was now a grandfather and that's important in family tradition. Like it or not, the baby, Ronald... not Ronaldo... just Ronald, was blood. Years later, Lucille had another kid - a daughter, Stephanie. Paolo and his family weren't invited to Calvino functions. Personally, I think they were better off."

"Still, that had to be awkward," Beryl said. "When you work with people, you hear about their holiday celebrations. You hear and tell all those 'water-cooler' anecdotes. How did Paolo take being left out?"

"It had to hurt, but he was a hard worker and must have impressed Antonio because my grandfather says that Antonio told him that if he went to church on Sundays and made his 'Easter Duty' - that means going to Confession and Communion - or, in other words, staying Catholic - he would inherit a share of the company equal to his brothers. Antonio had been Sole Proprietor of his company; but upon his death it would become a General Partnership when the three sons inherited it.

"But then one day in 1971, Antonio comes to my grandfather and asks him to be his attorney. Antonio wants to re-write his will. He had fired Paolo from his job with the company, and he also wanted Paolo to be cut out of the will completely."

"Did he say why he wanted Paolo out? And, why did he need a new attorney for a new will?"

"I don't know. I'm sure my grandfather knows, but he's not talking. And as far as becoming Calvino's new lawyer, why would he look that gift-horse in the mouth? - if I may use a western expression. In my whole life I have never looked in a horse's mouth."

"That you know of."

Martin began to giggle. "You're killin' me. I don't know why you can make me laugh so easily. Sometimes weeks go by and I don't have a single laugh. Then I'm around you and can't stop giggling. Ok. Stop making me laugh. This is important shit. Somebody's trying to kill my grandfather and you know how I feel about my Pop Pop."

"I do, indeed. Go on."

"So, out of the blue, in 1971, Antonio asks my grandfather to draw up a new will that completely disinherits Paolo. Well, Paolo and his wife and kids got the standard one thousand dollars each to show that they hadn't been left out through an oversight. At this point, everybody's still alive. Antonio had just fired Paolo, and Paolo took it hard and had to be treated for depression. I don't think Paolo knew that Antonio had written a new will. I think he just thought that he only lost his job with the firm because a few months later Antonio died and when the will was read and Paolo heard that all he was getting was that thousand dollars, he fell apart. Total despair and despondency. He took his family down to Mexico and committed suicide."

"How did he kill himself?"

"He filled his pockets with stones and walked into the Pacific. South of Tehuantepec."

"I know the town. It's on the Pacific side near Guatemala. The wind is fierce there. The ocean is called the Mar de Muerte. That's an odd place to commit suicide." She reconsidered. "Well, maybe not."

"After the will was read, it had been impossible for Paolo Calvino to stay up here. He was humiliated. I think he went down to Mexico because he could stretch whatever money he had a whole lot farther. His mother gave him whatever money she could sneak to him. They didn't have the drugs then that they have now. Paolo had apparently been interested in Amerindian art and artifacts, and there was a dig going on down there. He knew a couple of the archeologists and thought they would hire him, but they didn't. Maybe that added to his depression."

"Did he leave a note?"

"He left two: a short note to Lucille and a poem he wrote. Lucille read the note. She said it compared her and the kids to his north, east, and south, and that he was going to his Lord who waited for him in the west. She tried to read the poem but she was hysterical and crying and couldn't remember more than a few words in a couple of lines. When the police searched the house after finding his body on the beach, they took all his papers to the station. She never got the note or the poem back. The police said they misplaced them."

"And that was forty years ago? How is it related to the attempts on your grandfather's life?"

"Good question. I'll get to it. So in 1971, old Antonio, who was by then a widower, left his entire estate to his sons Giovanni and Lorenzo. The Sole Proprietorship of Antonio became a General Partnership of Giovanni and Lorenzo. Fifty-Fifty. But within months Lorenzo got in big financial trouble and Giovanni bought him out. And Calvino Investments became, once again, a Sole Proprietorship.

"Giovanni only had one kid, a boy who had Down's Syndrome and died young. But as I've said, Lorenzo had five kids. Giovanni kept Lorenzo on as an executive and he also kept Lorenzo's five kids on the payroll. Only one of them took the job seriously and ever did any work - that was his youngest son, Dino.... Dean, who's a friend of mine. Dean is the only one who finished college and had a degree in business. The others went from school to school... here and in Europe. But they couldn't cut it anywhere. Party animals. Fashionistas. You know the type."

"*Ray Ban's* and Armani suits in the wild wild West."

"Are you ever gonna let me live that down? And my goddamned sunglasses were *Gucci* not *Ray Ban*."

"My point, exactly."

Martin looked at the ceiling and affected a look of frustration. "*And the hits just keep on comin'.*" He and Beryl both liked to quote *A Few Good Men.*

"At ease, Counselor. Continue the story."

"Nobody hears squat about Paolo's family - not about his wife Lucille, his son Ronald and daughter Stephanie. Paolo is forgotten. It's like they never existed. Years pass. *Now,*" Martin said emphatically, "here is where the real story begins. One day last August, Giovanni comes to my grandfather and asks him to write a new will. He previously had left everything to Lorenzo and his family. Now, he obviously tells my grandfather *why* he wants a new will... but my grandfather won't reveal it. My secretary told me that when Giovanni came out of the office he looked like hell... his eyes were swollen and he clearly had been crying. *The new will left everything to Paolo's family.* He did leave Dean - Lorenzo's son and my friend - some money and property. You can't imagine the impact of this. In family wars, this was a cruise missile aimed at the heart.

"Evidently, my grandfather thought that the will would meet with some resistance, as we say. He took precautions to defeat 'mentally incompetent' challenges to it. He had Giovanni given psychiatric examinations, a complete physical, and even an CAT scan of his brain to establish that he was completely sound in body and mind when he gave everything to Paolo's family. Incidentally, Ronald Calvino got married and had a son who I've played racqueball with. Ronny, Jr. I actually like the guy.

"But the point is that aside from the standard one thousand dollars to show that they hadn't been left out unintentionally, Lorenzo and four of his children got nothing. Calvino Investments would still be a 'Sole Proprietorship' and Ronald Calvino, Sr. - Paolo's kid - would be that 'Sole.'

"My grandfather drew up the will. Giovanni signed it and proceeded immediately to fire Lorenzo. He didn't have to give cause, he just said that he was considering a new, 'modern' form of management. Lorenzo was retirement-age anyway. He got a severance package - not particularly generous - but it enabled him to look as if leaving the company were his idea. Giovanni drew up a resignation letter for Lorenzo to submit. My grandfather actually prepared the document. Lorenzo signed it and took the deal. He says that Giovanni promised to leave his kids in place at the firm, but Giovanni fired them anyway - one after the other, all except Dean. He stayed on. In fact, Giovanni gave him a raise.

"And then suddenly Giovanni dies. He was flying to Italy for both a Columbus Day celebration and a farewell party - his wife was taking some weird kind of layman's Holy Orders... 'retiring with grace' in a cloistered convent. Anyway, Giovanni got an embolism on the plane and had a stroke and one thing led to another and in a few weeks he was dead in a hospital in Rome."

"Where is his wife now?"

"Still in the convent in Italy. Giovanni had already dumped a load of cash on her and the convent she entered. And if she ever changed her mind and came back out, he set up accounts for her here. So she's fixed for life which isn't saying much since she's pushing eighty.

"Two months ago, in November, there was a reading of Giovanni's will. My grandfather located all four of them: Lucille - Paolo's widow; Ronald and Stephanie, Paolo's kids; and Ronny Junior, Paolo's grandson. And naturally, Lorenzo and his family were all there, too. Ronny Junior came right away. The rest of Paolo's family came to town a couple of days later. My grandfather put them up at the Country Club. After the will was read, they moved into a company condo, which they also inherited. My grandfather sponsored Ronny Junior for membership in the country club we belong to. I had been playing racquetball with him... but that's beside the point--"

"Not necessarily. What was Ronny, Jr. doing or not doing that he was able to pick up and come to Chicago to play racquetball with the young, handsome scion of the Mazzavini dynasty?"

"He had a dead end job, he said. So... I guess he just quit it."

"Do you happen to remember who his employer was?"

"We emailed each other a couple of times before he got here. I'm sure it's in my computer at work. It was someplace in San... San Something... in California."

"San... something? In California! That ought to narrow it down to... what? Five or ten thousand towns or so. And your computer is where? Lying on your desk where anyone can pick it up or access it. You're treating this information too casually." She grinned and rubbed one index finger over the other. "Pisper shame on you, MM. The minute my back is turned..."

"Jesus! Give me a break!" Martin yelled. "Who knew that all this trouble over a will was going to happen?"

Beryl shot back. "Your grandfather knew! That's why he ordered those extra tests. And now he's in a hospital because what he feared has come to pass."

"You are one tough woman! All right. I should have paid more attention to what was going on. I'm sorry!"

"Good. What happened when the will was read? How did Lorenzo and his family take this 'reversal of fortune'?"

"Not well. They went crazy shouting and screaming, calling my grandfather names and accusing Dean of somehow betraying them. Everyone was accusing everyone else. It was crazy... wild... I thought they'd start throwing things. I had to call security."

Beryl started a new page in her tablet. "Be specific. How did Lorenzo react... what were his exact words?" She clicked on her ballpoint pen. "What was the date, time, and place?"

"It was the Monday after a long holiday weekend. Veteran's Day. 10 a.m. My grandfather's office."

Beryl looked up a 2011 calendar and found that Friday, November 11th, was Veterans' Day. "Would that have been Monday, November 14, 2011?"

"Yes. It would. Thank you for looking that up. You're a hard woman. Monday, November 14th. Lorenzo Calvino came into the room with his wife and four of his children. Dino Calvino came in a few minutes later, so the entire Lorenzo Calvino family was there.

"Then Lucille Price Calvino came in with her and Paolo's son, Ronald Calvino, Sr. He had been divorced years before and never remarried. He's a former mining engineer; but he got hurt somehow and decided to open a supply store for miners - out in Nevada. Lucille and Paolo's grandson Ronny Calvino, Junior, came in next to last.

"We were still waiting on Stephanie Calvino - Paolo's daughter. She never married. She has an executive position with some advertising agency in New York. She's a lot younger than her brother." He made a few notes in his own little blue tablet.

Beryl waited until he finished writing. "So, what did Lorenzo specifically say? I don't mean 'cursing somebody out' - but specific charges - including the profanity."

"He called Dino - his own kid - a traitor... worse than a traitor, he said. Dino profited from his betrayal, blah blah. His own son had sold him out. Well, he was going to get another attorney and contest the will.

10

Dino was living in the clouds if thought that he was going to get away with it.

"Lorenzo's four other kids said that they were going to contest the will and Dino should never show his face around their houses again."

"How did the Paolo Calvino family react to all the craziness?"

"They said nothing at all. They just listened."

"What did Lorenzo mean when he said that Dino *had sold him out?*"

"I don't know. But that's exactly what he said." He made a note in his tablet.

"Tell me more about Giovanni's widow."

"She was in a convent. It was one of those Italian religious institutions that have been around since Tiberius or Constantine... whoever. She renounced all claims to the Calvino money and, as I've said, in exchange Giovanni had given her and the institution a nice hunk of change. When Giovanni went to Italy for that - I don't know what they call it - a 'going away' party for her, all the documents had already been executed and recorded. All the monies had been transferred. Giovanni just didn't make it to the party. She was not present at the reading of the will."

"Tell me about the attempts on your grandfather's life," Beryl said, "and then bring me up to date... where things stand as of this moment."

"Ok," he said, holding up his tablet, "I did write this down." He began to read. "He was ice fishing in November... up in Minnesota. It was Friday, November 18th." He looked up to explain. "They cut a hole in the ice and drop a fishing line down it... and put these little huts over the hole and usually sit around and bullshit while they wait for a fish to bite. Usually they're too drunk to notice that they've caught something... but they have a good time. He was alone in his custom-made hut, waiting for some friends to arrive and he went out to get something from his SUV parked at lakeside, and the goddamned hut blew up. It was supposed to be a propane tank malfunction... but he never sued the company and part of a timing device was found a quarter mile away on the ice. He shut down any ATF investigation. Don't ask me why. I don't know. Besides, most of the evidence went down into the hole that was blasted in the ice.

"The next attempt occurred on Wednesday, November 23rd. He went to a reception for some politician and his drink was spiked. He collapsed and wound up having his stomach pumped. He said it was a stomach virus. He was in the hospital for three days. The hospital records are sealed... doctor-patient confidentiality.

"The next attempt was on the 30th of November. He was going to his tobacco shop when a car passed by and a bullet hit him in the shoulder. The cops said it was an ordinary drive-by shooting. At least that's what he told the police. He said the car that passed was full of kids. I made sure they kept the bullet and I have the complete ballistic report on the slug they took out of him. Fortunately it just lodged in a muscle. He was wearing a shearling jacket at the time and it hit through a double leather thickness at the shoulder seam and pad.

"The last attempt was January 1st, New Year's Day, a Sunday. He gave his driver the holidays off, so my grandfather was driving himself. A truck came up beside him on a two-lane blacktop that goes back to his house. It was dark but not late... maybe 8 p.m. He said that a truck had been behind him and then suddenly the truck floored it and pulled up along side him and turned into him, bumping him twice. He didn't lose control the first time, but the second time he skidded down into a ditch and actually rolled over."

"Has there been any attempt to break into his office files?"

"No... none that I know of."

"Bring me up to date on the will."

"Lorenzo hired another firm to contest the will. I don't know where the suit stands now.

"Lorenzo's family treats Dean as though he's got the plague. He's going nuts trying to get back into their good graces. He doesn't know what he's supposed to have done that made them so mad."

"But what do they hope to gain that's worth the risk of attempting to murder the lawyer?"

"I don't know! According to them, they aren't the ones who are trying to kill my grandfather. No... they say that it's Ronald Calvino who wants to silence him... to keep him from revealing the truth. They say Ronald lied to Giovanni, telling him about crimes Lorenzo supposedly committed. These lies induced Giovanni to remove Lorenzo from his will. They say that if these lies were made public, they would be able to prove them to be lies. But Ronald Calvino, obviously, does not want the truth to come out. And since my grandfather knows the truth, Ronald wants to silence him permanently."

"Ah... I can see what Lorenzo's trying to do. Your grandfather knows that what was told to Giovanni was true; and they don't want him around to be able to say that."

"Yes! They're determined to break the will. Just because Giovanni Calvino was of sound mind and body doesn't mean that he wasn't duped or coerced. If there were deception... a calculated manipulation of events... a dishonest act that induced Giovanni to alter his original will, then the will could be broken. The original will would be reinstated. Ronald would be out. Lorenzo would be in."

Martin sat back in his chair. "If they didn't have this provision in law, somebody could hold a gun to your head and force you to write a new will and then..."

"Bump me off?"

"Yeah," he laughed. "Bump you off. And if you were an old lady in a nursing home and I was the young stud attendant you had ..."

"A hankering for..."

"I was going to say, 'a mad passionate desire for' but 'hankering' will do."

"And you would induce me to write a new will and then bump me off?"

"Hell no! I'd leave it just as it was... and put you on steroids."

"Dream on, Boychick." Beryl laughed. "Ok. I'll have to start thinking of you as a pool boy with a long skimmer and a law degree. Was an executor named?"

"Sure..." he laughed again, "a retired judge, an old friend of Giovanni's, a devout Catholic."

"Is Lorenzo pressuring him?"

"He hasn't made a secret of the fact that Ronald Calvino's family are Methodists."

"Does your grandfather know that you've called me in to investigate?"

"Yes. I told him. He knows how worried I am about him, but he says that he will not provide you with any information. He will not cooperate in your investigation. But he's looking forward to seeing you again."

"What's your gut feeling about this whole mess?"

"It stands to reason that Lorenzo knows exactly why his brother Giovanni threw him out of the company and disinherited him. But he will have to fabricate a story that will convince the court that one of Paolo's heirs lied to Giovanni about Lorenzo. As you've said, the problem for Lorenzo is that my grandfather undoubtedly knows the reason that Giovanni disinherited Lorenzo. That means my grandfather is the only person around who will be able to say that Lorenzo's phony accusations against Ronald are pure bullshit. Worse, he can reveal and probably prove what the real story is. In other words, for Lorenzo to succeed in overturning the will, he's got to say how and why and who deceived Giovanni, and he's got to get rid of the one man who can contradict his fictitious tale.

"But... it could be somebody else. Somebody that we're not even thinking about. At first I thought it was definitely Lorenzo... but, in fact, I really don't know why Giovanni changed his will. For all I know it really could have been a lie he had been told. Then I began to suspect everyone. What do you do when you think you understand something but then have all sorts of doubts? I don't mean just professionally, but in your private life. What do you do if you're confused about a personal problem?"

"I consult the *I Ching*."

"You say that seriously."

"If you're a believer, then it is an enormous help. But it isn't your confusion about a will that's the problem. It's Massimiliano Mazzavini's life. And the source of the problem is that secret that Giovanni told him. Remember, Giovanni didn't just leave his money to charity. He was rectifying something. This is a clear and unambiguous expiation of guilt."

"How do you know that?"

"If any one of the seven members of Lorenzo's family had insulted him, he might have disinherited him, but not the others - and surely not replaced them all with someone who has been out of the picture for a generation. No. A radical step like the complete substitution of one set of heirs by previously disgraced members of the family, indicates an atonement for something Giovanni did... and that no doubt was what Antonio did to Paolo forty years ago - and then Giovanni perpetuated the mistreatment. We need to start by finding out whatever it was that happened back then that caused Antonio to cut Paolo out of his will. What old records do you have from that time?"

"What we have is stored in a professional file storage company."

"Do you have access?"

"Yes. I don't think my grandfather will issue any orders to them to prevent me from getting into the files."

"Well, let's not tell him that we're going to snoop there."

"First thing tomorrow?"

"Why not? By the way, what was old Antonio's cause of death?"

"A heart attack while he was sleeping."

"Ok. Time to get some zzz's. It's been a long day." Beryl stood up and picked up her purse and tote bag. "I've got to get some sleep."

"Wait a minute," Martin said, reaching for her arm. "As long as you're here, help me with a personal problem I don't know how to solve."

Beryl sat down again. "Sure. I didn't mean to brush it off before. I'm sorry. What's the problem?"

"I dated a girl. Everybody liked her. Everybody said I should get engaged. She wanted a ring. Her birthday was in the beginning of December. 'Get her a ring,' my mother said. My mom went into her jewelry box and gave me a ring my father gave to her. I said, 'Mom... I don't want to get engaged. I'm not ready to get married.' So my mother goes to the hairdresser's and says that she gave this sentimental diamond ring to me to give to this girl, and my mom is so thrilled because it's time I settled down. The girl hears about it and next thing I know people are congratulating me on my imminent marriage. 'Did I set a date?'"

"Tell me why you're reluctant to marry this girl."

"I don't know. She's beautiful. Nice. Educated. Sexy. Great family."

"What do you want more than you want a wife?"

"I want to be a good lawyer. Does that sound stupid? I want to make a mark the way my grandfather made a mark."

"And this girl takes up a lot of time that you need to make your mark?"

"Well... yes."

"I can give you the Zen point of view. Martin, problems such as you've described usually consist in the failure to establish an order of precedence in Persona hats. As a little kid, you need a mother and father, so you wear a Son Hat. Then you become socialized and you need friends, so you wear a Friend Hat. You need your profession to earn money and become a useful member of your community, so you wear a Lawyer's Hat. You get married and have to wear a Husband Hat; and if you have kids you have to wear a Daddy Hat. All these relationships with mother, friend, client, wife, son, teammate, colleague keep adding up. And each one makes demands on you. Worse, it's not enough to be a son, you have to be a *good* son, and a *good* friend, a *good* lawyer, a *good* husband, a *good* teammate. Good isn't want *you* think. Good is what *they* think. And they raise hell with you if you don't meet their criteria.

"You have problems because when you're being a good husband by taking your wife to the theater, you're being a lousy lawyer because you didn't work late preparing a brief. When you're being a good father by helping your son with his math before his big test, you're being a lousy teammate because you didn't show up for bowling. What you need to do is to establish an order of precedence and make it clear to these people what their place is in the order of things."

"I did. I told her - Claudia is her name - I wanted to concentrate on being a good lawyer. She couldn't see why I couldn't be both her husband and a good lawyer. 'Most lawyers are married and their wives are helpful to them,' she says."

"What makes you think you owe anyone an explanation? Don't complain and don't explain. You shouldn't have told her that you wanted to concentrate on being a good lawyer. You should have just said that it was impossible for you to consider marriage at this time and that you are unable to discuss it. An excuse invites an argument that you will lose. Part of you wants to argue, to dominate and get your own way... maybe make her squirm. That's not Zen. You need to rise above these emotional needs of yours. Stop the warfare. Claudia is fighting for a place in your order of precedence; and you've already determined that place. Your big mistake was in condescending to argue. Did you give her the ring?"

"Yes... but I told her it was just a gift. I wasn't ready to get engaged and married."

"Did you make it absolutely clear that it was not a gift in contemplation of marriage?"

"Yes. But she thinks that because I didn't want the ring back... and it was my mother's ring... that I still intend to marry her."

"Does she persist in acting like your *fiancée?*"

"Jesus. She calls to ask me whether she should wear a long or a short dress to an affair that I didn't even want to go to because I had too much work to do. I'd turn my phone off, and she'd call my secretary."

"Did you talk to your grandfather? Wait... let me tell you what he said. He probably said if it is this bad now, it will only get worse when she has a position in law, that is to say, when she is your legal wife. Then you will have lost your leverage to control her."

"Leverage! That is exactly what he said! How did you know that? 'You'll lose your leverage then... she's behaving herself now because she fears that if she goes too far, you'll break off the engagement.'"

"And you said, 'What engagement? I never got engaged!'"

"Exactly. But everybody around me thinks I'm engaged. My phone's been turned off all evening. But you're here. I'll show you." He took out his phone and let Beryl listen to the voice mails. There were five messages from Claudia, each more demanding than the next. She wanted to know if Martin still intended to take her to his Grandfather's birthday party on Saturday night. She wanted to know why Dino or Ronny, Jr. couldn't take that 'woman writer from Philadelphia.' I told everyone you're writing a biography of my grandfather. Nobody's supposed to know you're a P.I.

And then it's 'How do you expect me to get ready on time when you won't tell me what time.' And always it's 'Call me back.' It's driving me crazy. I don't know what to do. There's so much damned pressure put on me."

"Consult the *I Ching*. You need the old version by Wilhelm - he preserves that ambiguous text. Ambiguity is the essence of an oracular utterance."

"Oracle? It sounds crazy. Will the *I Ching* tell me what to do?"

"No. It can only confirm what you know you want to do and are only superficially confused. Then it will guide you. Ok. Here's how it works. You cast a hexagram - and it doesn't matter which hexagram you cast - if you study it for clues, you'll find what you're looking for. Your mind must be able to concentrate rationally. First, you have to be in the 'either/or' quandary, and you have to be able to consider the 'Judgment' dispassionately. Its ambiguity has a purpose. A traditional oracle is too brief to be of help. There's a famous oracular message. Around five hundred BC, King Croesus asked the oracle at Delphi if he should attack the Persians. His army was encamped on one side of a river and the Persians were on the other side. The oracle said, 'If you cross the river, you will destroy a great army.' Obviously he wanted to believe that this meant the Persians would be destroyed. It was an emotional response - and it was therefore worthless. It turned out to be his own great army that was lost. The *I Ching* is a superior oracle because it forces the person to examine the judgment. All right. Tear a page out of your tablet and write down the question. Don't tell me what it is. Just write it down and put it away."

Martin tore out a page and thoughtfully wrote the question.

"Fold it up, put it in your pocket, and take three coins out of your pocket."

Martin took out three dimes.

"Make a cup of your hands and shake them so that the coins tumble inside and then slap them down on the table. Heads is 2 - female; and tails is 3 - male. Some people say just the opposite. But it doesn't matter. You have to hold the coins, tumble them, and slap them down. You can't do it for someone else. Then you add the values of the three coins."

Beryl tore a sheet from her tablet and wrote on descending lines, 1,2,3,4,5,6. "Even is a broken line. Odd is a straight line. Some people say the opposite but it doesn't matter."

Martin threw 2 tails and 1 head, total: 3 + 3 + 2 = 8 even. Beryl showed him how to record the result for Line #6. She drew a broken line opposite #6 at the bottom, and on the same line at the side of the page wrote the number 8. "Now you do it for the next five lines and build the hexagram upwards. Tomorrow we'll pick up the Wilhelm/Baynes version of the *I Ching*. You'll look up the hexagram you finish drawing now. Study it. You don't need to discuss it. You'll find your answer. Just finish the other five lines, going up from the bottom. I'm going to take a shower and hit the sack."

Martin stayed at the kitchen table mumbling to himself as he tossed the dimes and recorded the lines and values. "Next 3 tails: 3 + 3 + 3 = 9 (odd) a straight line in number 5." He wrote the number 9 on the side. Next he tossed 3 tails again = 9, (odd) a straight line in #4. Next 2 heads and one tail: 2 + 2 + 3 = 7 (odd) a straight line in #3. He tossed 3 heads = 2 + 2 + 2 = 6 (even) a broken line in #2. Finally he tossed 2 tails and one head = 3 + 3 + 2 = 8 (even) a broken line at the #1 top. He folded the paper and put it in his pocket. And memorized the lines:

$$-\ -$$
$$-\ -$$
$$--$$
$$--$$
$$--$$
$$-\ -$$

The next day, when he consulted the *I Ching*, he would match the hexagram he had drawn to the chart at the back of the book and discover that he had drawn the horoscope #32, *Heng, Chen over Sun*; The Arousing over the Gentle; Thunder over Wind = "Duration." When he turned to #32 and slowly read the oracular pronouncement, he would think that a few thousand years of oriental wisdom had leapt from the pages into his mind.

WEDNESDAY, JANUARY 4, 2012

Before Martin and Beryl could enter the *Mazzavini O'Brian Mazzavini* storage vault it was necessary to follow the vault's regulations. According to protocol, a formal intention to enter the vault had to be filled out and left with M.O.M.'s office manager. A copy of the notice would be given to the guard at the vault and he would check identification and call the office manager to verify it. Then the visitor was allowed to punch in the security code to the vault. The security it afforded more than offset the inconvenience.

At ten o'clock Thursday morning, Martin and Beryl, both wearing casual western clothing, entered his ultra modern high rise office and smiled their way through the few dozen turned heads who stared with disbelief and consternation as they passed. "This disapproval is all my fault," Beryl whispered. "I forgot to bring those bolo ties with scorpions encased in Lucite."

Martin paused at the door to his office. "The moment my back was turned... you forgot... *forgot* to make a note." He began to laugh at his fellow disapproving lawyers. He finally managed to say, "*All that disdain could have been admiration, if only you remembered to write down 'Bring scorpion bolos'!*"

Beryl looked back at the office members who were still staring at them. "You ought to go back and apologize for offending their esthetic sensibilities."

"I ought to get a fucking barrel of scorpions and dump it on them. *Entré, si'l vous plait.*" With a sweeping gesture, Martin showed Beryl his office.

"It's almost exactly as I imagined it," she said.

"What?" he said, expecting an insult.

"I'm gratified to see the black leather and chrome. What a unique way to decorate a lawyer's office! If a picture of this gets out, other lawyers are gonna copy it. But no matador on velvet? No Elvis? No kids with big eyes? Where is your taste, man? Complete the job!"

Martin Mazzavini laughed and quoted a line from, *A Few Good Men*. *"Have I done something to offend you?"*

Beryl stared back at "the suits" who were watching them through the glass wall. "Tell them we're going undercover at a rodeo. And, could you ask your secretary to print out a list of newsworthy events for 1969, 1970, and 1971. If she can find a list of financially significant events for that time, we want that, too."

Still laughing, Martin ordered his secretary to fill the request. He then turned and asked Beryl why she wanted the information.

"Because we want to get the feel of those years. What was the big buzz in 1970 and 71. That is the approximate time Antonio Calvino decided to take his business to your grandfather."

The printouts were ready by the time he filled out the form to enter the stored files' vault.

On their way to the vault, Martin stopped in a bookstore and purchased a copy of the *I Ching*.

Calvino Investments' 1970 and 1971 tax returns each took up an entire drawer. "Where shall we start?" Martin asked.

"Do you know the definition of a weed?"

"Yes, Ma'am. You told me last year. A weed is a plant that is out of place."

"Gotcha'."

"The Vietnam War; the Beatles breakup; Aswan High Dam; Kent State shootings. Those were the popular events. Aside from Paolo's anti-war sentiments, I don't imagine that any of them figured in this. What were the major financial interests of Calvino?" Beryl asked.

"I know what they are now and I'm told they really haven't changed: lumber; oil; war materiel - mostly dry goods like uniforms, parachutes, backpacks; frozen foods; paper products; and the Asian markets. Calvino Investments is considered very conservative. They didn't get into the big electronics' market... none of that dot.com phase. It was a sort of 'If it ain't broke, don't fix it' philosophy. They made a steady profit and especially during all the Wall Street and Vatican scandals their clients didn't lose a dime. Some people like the comfort of security and some like the excitement of risk."

"Then they've been consistent. So look for any investments or expenses put in by Lorenzo or Paolo that seem out of the ordinary. Giovanni bought Lorenzo out at the same approximate time that Antonio disinherited Paolo. Within a year, right? So look for the reason that caused both of these events. The reason has to have a paper trail."

"There's a section of photocopied documents devoted to 1969." He looked through it. "This file was made for reference purposes. It's for Antonio Calvino who filed as the Sole Proprietor of the business." He returned the file to the drawer. "And here are photocopies of his returns for the fiscal year 1970. Nobody in our firm had anything to do with these tax returns. We have the copies also just for reference." He looked through them and shook his head. "Nothing in these suggests anything unusual." He replaced the file and removed a file that contained a copy of Antonio's will. "This will, which my grandfather wrote in October 1971, provides for the equal division of Antonio's assets between Lorenzo and Giovanni and that a General Partnership be created at the time of Antonio's death. Paolo received one thousand dollars." He returned the document to the file drawer.

"All right," he said. "Let's look through the tax returns of Fiscal Year 1971 which were filed in March of 1972." He removed half a dozen files and made a stack of them on the vault's desk. He looked through one file after another, handing them to Beryl to look through and then replace. "I don't see anything that looks like a weed. He bought out Lorenzo and the General Partnership reverted to a Sole Proprietorship with Giovanni Calvino being the sole owner. Lorenzo, 'and all his heirs and assigns,' irrevocably relinquish their interests in the partnership for... wow... forty million dollars - which in those days was a whole lot more than it is today. So Lorenzo got $40 million. What the hell did he do with forty million dollars? It couldn't have had a negative effect on the business since Giovanni kept him on."

"When did the buyout occur?" Beryl asked.

"November, 1971."

"Look through the supplemental sheets. Somebody had to buy something... an airline ticket to a place unrelated to any of their financial interests. Something out of the ordinary. An employee contract terminated at a significant cost to the partnership. A new department created and then deconstructed. Look through Paolo's expenses. Maybe he managed to divert money to something. I don't know. Look!"

Martin looked at the business expenses Paolo had submitted for reimbursement. "There aren't many of them. He didn't have an executive position. He did some traveling... it's called 'troubleshooting' for union disputes... attending a conference for regulation changes regarding deforestation... some modest hotel accommodations. A subscription for Aviation Week." He looked up. "Why would he put a subscription for Aviation Week in as a company expense?"

Beryl shrugged. "Maybe because he thought that the company was going to get involved in Aviation. What happened in that time frame that might induce the company to invest in Aviation? Moon landings. The Vietnam War. We'll have to check that out. Keep reading." She made a note in her tablet.

"Within a week of getting the magazine subscription, Paolo submitted a $27 request for reimbursement for Geological Survey maps. What would these maps have been for?" Beryl asked.

"I have no idea," Martin said. "The investment company would have the receipts that back up all these expense sheets and they're just too old to be around anywhere. Let's just put it on the list of peculiarities that require explanation."

Paolo's monthly statement for April, 1971, contained travel and miscellaneous expenses for "scouting sites for branch office." There were no receipts for food, travel, shelter to substantiate the five thousand dollar miscellaneous expense. There is a note by Lorenzo, *supportive documents inadvertently destroyed.'* They were so meticulous about their expense sheets that I guess they thought they could get away with that 'the dog ate my homework' excuse."

"When was Stephanie born?"

"She was born in 1970... February."

"Could it have anything to do with her birth?" Beryl wondered.

"Maybe this is what the mystery is all about. Ronald Jr. was born in 1957 but Stephanie was born in 1970. That's a big jump in time. Let's check into that, too. There are so many possibilities... but we can eliminate most of them if we see if they have the same parents. They didn't have DNA in those days." Then he returned to the expense sheet. "Why," he asked, "would anybody send Paolo to Ottawa to scout out a branch office? I've never heard a word about any expansion into a foreign country."

"We can check that, too," Beryl said. "Let's keep looking."

Martin reviewed the remaining expense reports that Paolo had submitted. There were only skimpy requests for reimbursement in May, June, July, and August, which was the last expense account sheet for Paolo.

It was time to get lunch. "My eyes are starting to see double," Martin said. "And I want to look up what the oracle told me to do."

"The oracle isn't going to tell you to do anything. It will strengthen your resolve to do what, in your heart, you really want to do." She returned all the files and locked the cabinets and handed Martin his keys. "I think we have enough to work on now," Beryl said. "If we come up empty with the magazine subscription, the kids born so far apart in time, the branch office expenses, and the inadvertent destruction of supportive receipts, we can start looking through Lorenzo's expenses."

A cold and overcast winter day had driven away Lakeshore Drive's heralded blue and green beauty. The trees were bare and Lake Michigan's water was grey. It was the kind of dreariness that turned thinking into brooding. There was movement all around them but the car windows were shut tight and the noise that should have accompanied the movement was absent. The unnatural silence was more disturbing than all the motor, horn, and "rubber on the road" noises ever could have been.

"I feel like I'm on a train," Beryl said. "Maybe it's more like a silent film and I'm tied down on the tracks."

"I don't have any of that ominous danger piano music," Martin said. "But after we talked about opera in Tucson, I went out and got *La Fanciulla del West* by Puccini. I forgot to load it into the iPod."

"What? You didn't remember to make a note in your blue tablet? *La Fan D. Wst. Puch.*"

Martin laughed. "Without a nag constantly reminding me to make notes to remember, I fell into evil ways. I miss Tucson," Martin confessed. "This weather's a killer up here. If I didn't have this fantastically successful law practice..."

"How is your practice going? Have you officially switched to criminal law?"

"I am still buried under all my victory paperwork. You can't imagine the amount of work I'm doing mopping up after that big Arizona win. My secretary - the one who used to have nothing to do - now has an assistant. I had to go back and forth to Phoenix and Tucson so often that it started to kill me... changing clothes, changing clothes. I now understand and appreciate cowboy fashion. You take your jacket off when it's warm. You put your jacket on when it's cold. My whole summer wardrobe was a disaster. All my linen suits crinkled up so much sitting on a plane - the goddamned top of my socks showed! I said, 'To hell with it,' and went out and bought a half dozen jackets like my new idol, Gerry Spence, wears. We successful trial lawyers have a persona to maintain. I started to wear my western stuff when I went down. Every now and then I wear western clothes into the office. You saw the response. The first time they thought I was going to a costume party. The second time they laughed. My grandfather reminded everyone about the size of the fee we earned and said that if they ever earned half that fee in any one case, *he'd* wear cowboy clothes."

"Did you actually go to trial in Arizona?"

"No. The 'sons a bitches' met my terms. Every goddamned one of them caved. My threat to expose all unless they all complied - complete unanimity - worked. It actually worked. They all settled out of court! So I still haven't won a capital case. Goddamned cowards."

Beryl laughed. "Ingrates! You make 'em pay through the nose and they still won't give you the satisfaction of drillin' 'em a new one in court. No wonder you've turned mean."

He exited the highway and drove to a restaurant. "I called earlier for reservations. I hope they don't have a dress code."

"Wear your scorpion bolo tie. You'll scare the *maitre d.* into giving you the best table in the joint."

They ordered lunch, and as they waited for their order to arrive, Martin studied the hexagram he had cast: #32, *Heng. Duration.*

"God damn!" He kept muttering approvingly. "Jesus, I can't believe this. It's perfect."

"I don't want to know. I'm not your Dao priest."

"After we eat, let's go visit my grandfather."

"Please don't burden that man with the terrifying thought that you, his great protector, are resorting to the *I Ching* to keep him safe."

"All I want to do is teach him how to use the book. They had another copy in the bookstore. Maybe I'll swing by and get it for him. He'll like it. He likes stuff like this. The man's uncanny. He sees things most people miss."

At the hospital, Massimiliano Mazzavini was taking a nap. Beryl and Martin sat and waited for him to awaken, but the old man had stayed up late watching movies on his laptop and was catching up on the night's sleep that he had missed.

They left to "drop in on" the new head of Calvino Investments.

Ronald Calvino, appointed temporarily by the executor to sit at the "Sole Proprietor's" desk at Calvino Investments, his son, Ronny Jr., his cousin

Dino Calvino, and the company's comptroller all sat in Ronald's office discussing financial practices.

Beryl had insisted that they not call ahead for an appointment. She explained, "If someone is bugging his calls and knows we're coming, he or she can simply turn off the device and thwart my scanner. It's also best that we look a little bizarre on the 'hokey' side since high tech surveillance - if you can call my scanner high tech, which it is not - is the last thing people suspect of people who appear to be bizarre and 'hokey.'"

"We should have dressed up as Amish farmers," Martin said. "American Gothic."

"Why?" she asked. "You look perfectly bizarre and hokey in that suede fringe jacket and those python boots... even without the scorpion bolo."

"They're stuck with me in my office. But this is a high class firm, especially now that Lorenzo's gone. I talk to Ron often, but on the phone... not in person."

The receptionist at Calvino's executive office suite viewed them with alarm as they approached. Beryl whispered, "Tell her we're soliciting for Victims of Ramrod Abuse," a remark which struck Martin funny. He began to giggle as he stood at the receptionist's desk. Beryl also had to turn away and stifle the urge to laugh.

Without having been summoned, a security guard walked purposefully to the receptionist's desk. "Any problem here?" he asked.

"We'd like to see Mr. Ronald Calvino," Beryl said.

"Do you have an appointment?" the receptionist asked, her voice edged with amusement.

"No," Beryl said, reaching into Martin's shirt pocket to remove one of his business cards. "Tell Mr. Calvino that his attorney is here." She gave the receptionist the card.

The woman cautiously held the card by its edges and called Calvino's secretary. She then nodded to the security guard who nevertheless thought it prudent to escort "Mr. Mazzavini and friend" back to Calvino's office.

Martin and Beryl were ushered into the sumptuous waiting room of Calvino Investments' sole proprietor.

Ronald Calvino came out of his office immediately. He looked like a man who had been a castaway on an island for years and was greeting the first human beings who had come ashore. He had spent two thirds of his life being what he was: an intelligent but homespun mining engineer who had gone into the retail mining supply business. He did not gross in one year what his new business netted in a few hours.

"How ya' doin'?" Martin asked. "Getting the knack of Hi-Fi?" They shook hands.

"High finance is not low finance, writ large," Ronald said, laughing. "A balance sheet is not necessarily a *balance sheet*. The chief's teepee and Buckingham Palace just ain't the same thing however much they are the residences of leaders."

He was not "at home" wearing tailored suits, but he wore them well. He was in his fifties but his body had the muscular hardness of a man in his twenties. Ron Calvino rode horses and he worked out at a gym regularly. He did not drink, smoke, or eat meat for he had "given them up" when his wife was gravely ill with ovarian cancer. He had prayed and made a vow that if God allowed her to recover, he would deprive himself of alcohol, tobacco, and meat to show the depth of his gratitude. She recovered and he kept his word, even though she eventually divorced him. His contract with God was inviolable, although few in his new cosmopolitan surroundings would have understood a supplicant's "homespun" accommodation. It struck Beryl immediately that however much he displayed Nevada attitudes to life, the presentation was merely the patina that covered Roman dignity and charm. He could have been Cicero standing in the doorway with a laurel wreathe and toga. "Look at them boots!" he yelped. "God Damn! Are they real python?"

"Yep," Martin said, raising his boot-cut pants' leg to show off the entire boot.

"Must have cost a fortune! Come on in! Where didja' get 'em?"

"Tucson."

"I've got a half dozen pair of good boots... but none like them. I didn't think we were supposed to wear them in here. I just spent a shitload of money buying tailor-made suits."

Beryl whispered as she signaled to Ronald, "Keep talking." She raised her scanner to show him the device.

Martin tried to be helpful. "Well, a lot of places have what they call 'Casual Friday.' The office staff can wear anything they want... anything reasonable," he said. "Maybe you could institute that here and wear some of your boots. Only now you can afford to buy genuine snake or ostrich. I also have a pair of ostrich boots."

Beryl checked the scanner as she circled the room. She entered the adjoining bathroom and summoned Martin and Ronald, indicating that they keep talking about boots. She selected a pick from the small envelope of lock picking tools she carried in her tote bag and opened the paper towel dispenser. Inside the lid was taped a voice-activated digital recorder. She returned to the office and motioned them to follow her out of the office - as she showed them the stage direction she had written in her notebook. "Exit Laughing."

Calvino grinned and said, appropos of nothing, "My wife dared me about that... but I didn't fall into that trap."

"In other words," said Martin precociously, "you didn't practice what you breached!"

The three laughed at the supposed humor. Beryl said, "There's a name for men like you... but we ladies don't discuss it in mixed company." More phony laughter.

"How long will this take?" Calvino asked Beryl as he stopped at his secretary's desk.

Beryl invented an appointment and made up a plausible account for their absence. "He's in the building. I'll call before we get on the elevator. If he's busy talking to someone, we can come back here and wait for his call. If he can see us, half an hour at most."

"Did you get that?" Calvino asked his secretary.

She smiled. "You'll be back anywhere between three and thirty minutes."

They took the elevator to the ground floor, exited the building, and took a cab to the nearest electronic supply store.

Beryl advised Calvino, "Go in and buy a digital recorder that is a duplicate of this one. Be sure to get new batteries. We can take this one and listen to everything that's on it. It looks to me to have five channels that will record two hours of actual speech." She and Martin waited in the cab.

Calvino returned in a few minutes with an exact copy of the recorder. They told the cab to return to the office building.

"Is there anything that you talked about during the last three days that you don't want anyone to hear?" Beryl asked.

"I don't want anyone overhearing any of it," Calvino said indignantly.

Martin explained, "Of course you don't. But if you want to know who is listening to your conversations you have to let him think you're unaware of what he's doing. Turn on your new player and put it in the towel dispenser. Take this old one and just listen to the conversations. You can plug in earphones. Wherever there is a call that is of particular significance that you don't want others to hear, erase it."

"Yeah.. I get it. I'm just so shocked by this. Who the hell would do it?" Calvino shook his head.

"Did you have a new telephone installed when you first took over?" Beryl asked.

"Yes... there had been an ordinary four-line phone on the desk; and at my secretary's suggestion we had a cordless phone installed."

"I would suspect her of being in your uncle Lorenzo's employment. But that is simply a suspicion. We'll see who fetches the tape when we dust for prints in a few days. Meanwhile, say nothing to anyone. You don't know who else is bugged. Anything that's important should be discussed in a Sauna."

"Something like this has never happened to me before," Calvino said.

"It happens much more than you think," she said. "I'd like you to buy a Wave radio and plug it in immediately. If you're watching TV, you can turn it off. But don't let the room go silent. Continue to talk to people exactly as you've been doing. And tell no one about any of this. By no one, we mean no one. That means your family, too. Serious attempts have been made on Mr. Mazzavini's life. You may be next. Any information you give someone puts that person in jeopardy."

"I understand... and I understand what my uncle Lorenzo is trying to do. How long will this trouble go on?"

"If you want to try to secure a lifetime of financial prosperity you must suffer through this indignity now. I'm not an electronic surveillance specialist. If I thought you were being seriously bugged, I'd call one in. But this device is an amateur job. The phone is also standard eavesdropping. Still, the best way to prevent anyone overhearing what you're saying is not to say it. The best way to prevent anyone from reading private correspondence is not to write it. Every time you get the uncontrollable impulse to start talking or typing, rub your head and whistle Dixie. You don't have to justify your reasons... you don't even have to state them. You are the sole owner. The top of the food chain. So stop communicating things that ought to stay in your mind until you decide to activate your thoughts. If you need advice, call your assistant and take him out to a busy restaurant and talk to him."

"Look at me," Martin said whimsically. "When she's around, I'm her slave. Abject servility."

Calvino looked at him and laughed, his mood lightening. "Anything you say," he said, relenting. He turned to Beryl, "Are you undercover or does everyone know you're an investigator?"

"I think for this job Martin has told people I'm a writer.. doing a biographical account of..." she paused to refine the imposture, "two extraordinarily successful Italians... Mazzavini and Calvino - that is, Massimiliano Mazzavini and Giovanni Calvino. You may be asked to furnish old photographs or fictitious anecdotes."

"I'll do everything I can to help you to write a book about my uncle Giovanni and his good friend, Massimiliano Mazzavini." Ronald grinned.

"Let's meet again for dinner to discuss how you made out and whether you learned anything that might help to solve this case," Beryl suggested.

They entered the building, took the elevator to the 80th floor and re-entered Calvino's office, talking about the fictitious time that Giovanni taught Ronald how to swim.

Beryl thoroughly wiped down the paper dispenser lid, cartridge, and player.

They planned to meet for dinner at a place Beryl would pick when they met outside the building at five o'clock.

As they walked to the parking garage, Martin asked, "Would you do me a favor and sweep my office?"

"It's not bugged," she said.

"How do you know?" he asked.

"Because I swept it when we were there earlier. And your apartment is clean, too."

"I paid five hundred bucks last week for a guy to sweep my office. I should've consulted 'The Book.'"

They had dinner at a Lakeside cafe. Ronald Calvino had not been able to assimilate the events that had recently disrupted his life. "A few weeks ago I was minding my own business, tending my store in Nevada. One day there are men with certified letters telling me to contact Massimiliano Mazzavini in Chicago... that I had just inherited a fortune from my uncle. It made no sense. He had many other living relatives. And a few weeks ago I heard that I want to kill Mazzavini because I don't want people to find out why my Uncle Giovanni made my mother, sister, son, and me his heirs. And this ain't like killing the messenger. This is something worse. And I don't know what that is."

"We can't solve that problem," Beryl said, "until we figure out what happened in Chicago forty years ago. Your father's fate seems to be the key to all of this; and we need to ask you some questions. Tell us whatever you know. Let's understand... our primary interest is not in your inheritance or your father's misfortune. We're trying to protect Mr. Mazzavini. By doing that, we'll be protecting you, too. The point is that Martin is your attorney and I'm his agent so privilege applies. Nothing you say can be repeated by him or me. So try to answer as completely as possible.

"You were a teenager when your father spent his last year with the investment company. What was he interested in that made him buy Geologic Survey maps.... or take out a subscription to Aviation Week? Do you remember anything about his going to Canada for a week in April supposedly to look for a place for a branch office? Is there anything unusual about your sister's birth? There's a big gap in time between your ages. In short, we need to know anything that can shed light on whatever happened back then that made your grandfather disinherit your father."

"That's a long time ago. I was a kid and wasn't that close to the business. About Aviation Week magazine, I don't know anything. But I do know that my dad gave me a model of the Concorde that I put together."

"Did you normally work on model planes? Was he interested in getting a pilot's license? Was the company interested in investing in an airline company?"

"As a matter of fact I never made any models before. The Concorde was the first one. It came with a kind of spire mounting... so that when I was finished with the plane I hooked it on top of the spire with its nose up - as though it were in flight. I don't know what happened to it."

"Do you recall a group of Geological Survey maps your dad got?"

"No. I know what they are... we use them in the mining industry. But I honestly can say I don't remember anything about maps back then."

"What do you know about a trip to Ottawa to look for a new site for a branch office? Investment houses don't usually branch out into foreign countries - at least not by scouting out a new location site on which to build an office. That sounds just plain wrong. Yet, he scouted various locations. Do you remember that he went away in the Spring?"

"Oh, Yes, yes, yes. But that was a medical problem. He was having physical problems - serious ones - when my Mom drove him up to Canada. She took the baby... my little sister. I remember that. I stayed in Chicago with a kid I went to school with. My Mom gave them money for a week's room and board. I can't remember the kid's name... but I remember staying there."

"Was your father depressed at that time?"

"No. It was a physical problem. And I do remember wondering why he seemed so happy. He had been injured... somehow. He was hurt bad enough for him to get treatment, but it wasn't psychological. Not then. Later he was severely depressed. You know that ultimately he killed himself."

"Yes. We're sorry that we have to ask these questions especially in consideration of the suicide."

"There was a very long time between your birth and your sister's birth.. a dozen years or so. Do you know of any reason why the second birth occurred so long after the first?"

"No... not really. I was a kid just going into high school. I think my mom had some female problems. But then she had surgery and she also got some medicine that gave her terrible fever-like symptoms. She got what she called 'hot flashes' - they scared me. But she said they helped her to become pregnant. She had wanted another baby for a long time. But I learned this later on. I remember being the only kid in school that had a baby sister."

Beryl turned to Martin. "It sounds like maybe she had endometriosis--"

"Yes!" Ronald exclaimed. "I heard that term. She also told my sister not to wait too long to get pregnant because when you get older, there's a bigger risk."

"That would have made it difficult for her to get pregnant. A woman gets a funny growth of tissue that is fed by estrogen. What they do is give you male hormones or something... you go into menopause for lack of estrogen. Did anyone ever doubt that this was her problem? What I mean is was there ever any gossip that intimated that perhaps your sister was someone else's child?"

"No. None that I ever heard of. I don't know that I would have heard such gossip back then. But there might have been such talk. Mr. Mazzavini had both my sister and me take DNA tests... and my mother, too. Last summer when he made the will, he had my Uncle Giovanni take one, too. That may have been pre-emptive... you know, to negate any rumors that were still floating around. There wasn't any way to get my father's DNA. The hospital in Ottawa would certainly not have any tissue samples from 1971 and my dad was buried in Tehuantepec. Did anyone suggest that some paternity issue might be motivating me to try to harm Mr. Mazzavini?"

Beryl shook her head. "At this point, we don't know anything. Nothing would surprise us. Who has the DNA reports now?"

"Mr. Mazzavini."

Martin shrugged. "Nobody told me anything about DNA tests."

"I guess your grandather thinks that it is not your case. He probably doesn't want you to get involved in it. Tell me... what does your father think about all this?"

"My dad and Lorenzo's oldest son were golf-course buddies... nothing more. He doesn't say much one way or the other."

"Is it all right," Ronald asked, "if I change the subject now? What do I do about my secretary and the cleaning lady who comes into my office?"

"Tomorrow... or if you go back to your office tonight, leave your office unlocked. Just don't leave any important papers in there."

"Right now I'm getting lessons in ownership. I had some accounting classes when I was in college and I can just about read a balance sheet and a 'profit and loss' statement. Otherwise, I know nothing."

"Were you told how money was disbursed when Lorenzo was there? Did he have absolute 'power of the purse'?

"No. And that surprised me. The comptroller said that previously any check over one thousand dollars had to be signed by Giovanni Calvino. Which is another way of saying that Lorenzo had access to the petty cash fund and that's all. Giovanni didn't just rubber-stamp the payouts. In my current lessons I repeatedly hear, 'Mr. G. wanted it done this way... and Mr. G. wanted it done that way.' And the comptroller says, 'I'd give Mr. G. the reports and he would..' - it was never Lorenzo. So Lorenzo was CEO with a limited credit card."

Martin said, "This shows a lack of confidence in Lorenzo. This is good to know now… in case there's a fight over the will. Maybe my grandfather doesn't know this."

"You can ask him when you pick him up tomorrow," Beryl suggested.

Ronald, still alarmed about the bugging incident in his office, wanted to know who was conducting the surveillance. "When will you come again for the fingerprints on the tape recorder?"

"Sunday. The big birthday party is Saturday night. If someone other than your secretary or the cleaning lady is tending the recording, then Friday or Saturday night would be an ideal time to get the tape. What we need also is to talk to your mother. Where is she staying?"

"The company owns a condo and Judge Callaghan, the executor, gave her permission to move into it while the will is being probated."

Beryl took down the address and asked Calvino to get his mother on the phone. He did and Beryl got on the line and asked if she would meet her for brunch in the morning to discuss a biography that was being written about, "the man who willed you his company and the lawyer who was his friend and confidant." The meeting was arranged for ten o'clock the following morning in the condo lobby. "We can decide where to go when we discuss what we feel like eating.

"The condo," she explained to Ronald, "is probably bugged. You cannot telephone your mother and tell her anything on the phone. I'll tell her what I'm actually doing when she and I are alone in a public restaurant. And if you go to her residence, you cannot tell her anything inside. Take her out for a walk."

"Would it be permissible for me to get one of those sweeping things?"

"Of course. But don't alarm your mom. And tell her not to discuss anything on the phone and not to say, 'Ronald tells me that this phone may be bugged so I can't discuss anything on the phone with you.'"

Everyone laughed. "That's something that I would do," Ronald said. "I'm just not used to intrigue."

"It will soon become second nature to you," Beryl said.

Martin removed his little blue tablet from his shirt pocket and showed it to Ronald Calvino. "My grandfather and I have all kinds of gadgets. When I first learned to use these little paper spiral tablets, I was convinced I'd never revert to the old fashioned electronic tablets. But then I backslid. I got lazy. I had all these gadgets and they are like Sirens singing to drunken sailors. So for awhile I went back to the battery operated stuff. But one day I misplaced my iPad and I panicked. I thought it had been stolen. I found it two days later and went back to my little tablet. The dominatrix, here," he pointed at Beryl, "doesn't know that I also bought a Gregg shorthand book. I'm getting pretty good at it. One of the hotshot lawyers in our firm saw me writing in the tablet and laughed in my face. Then his attaché case was switched in a restaurant. He had so much data in his electronic toys. He nearly had a nervous breakdown. He lost his next case so badly that he almost lost his job. I'm serious. He's on probation. I laughed at him and waved my little cryptic blue tablets. They were so goddamned cryptic even I couldn't understand what I had written - which is why I learned Gregg. I never discuss a case on a portable phone. If you're smart you'll go back to your old landline. I did. I use the electronic stuff for social email and solitaire. Just go down to a Salvation Army Thrift shop and buy yourself one of those old telephones... the kind you can unscrew the ends of the receiver to make sure they're not bugged."

"And here's another caveat," Beryl added, "in case you frequent the same restaurant or end of the bar at the 19th hole, or have a company jet, or hotel suite, or limousine, just remember that a chauffeur, maitre d', chambermaid, bartender, barber are all ordinary people. They can be hired by your Uncle Lorenzo and they can pump you for information or report comments they've overheard. Don't ever get the idea that only government agencies or private detectives will spy on you. College kids will pay their tuition by hacking into your equipment or follow you around to record your cellphone or portable phone calls. Secretaries can get angry with you and spite you by selling your secrets. So can your wife and kids. If you don't speak it, nobody can hear it. If you don't write it, nobody can read it. Record only what must be recorded. Talk is a precious commodity. Don't squander it."

"You're supposed to stand up and salute and say, *"Ja, meine Königin."* Martin grinned and called for the check.

"Well, what do you think?" Martin asked after Beryl had once again swept his apartment.

"It will all fit together... somehow. Some of it sounds so violent. Paolo is injured but happy. The injuries are treated in Canada and covered up with some 'new branch office site' story. There was no attempt, apparently, to file insurance claims for his treatment... which might be another reason why he crossed the border to receive treatment. That is just too weird. And then, Lorenzo got himself into such debt that he had to sell his half of the business to his brother - who evidently wouldn't give him a loan. He has to pay up even if it means selling his interest in that gold mine of an investment company."

"That," said Martin emphatically, "sounds like loan sharking to me."

"Yes. That's exactly what it sounds like. And loan sharks would be the kind of people who would injure Paolo; but Paolo wasn't the one who owed them the money."

"When I pick up my grandfather tomorrow I'll discuss getting him to visit the Italian American Club for lunch. Maybe he can learn about those loan sharks. If he's not up to it, I'll go to the public library and research Mafia news for 1971 or thereabouts. Or maybe I can find a retired FBI agent who remembers the time. Something went on. Something big..."

THURSDAY, JANUARY 5, 2012

Mrs. Paolo Calvino wore no makeup and combed her hair back into a braid that she coiled at the nape of her neck. She wore no jewelry except a gold wedding band and a gold chain and cross around her neck. She was as erect in her carriage as any woman, of any age, that Beryl had ever seen. Regal, in fact. When she approached Beryl's table, she extended her hand and Beryl stood up to shake it. Beryl smiled admiringly.

"You are looking at me so strangely," Lucille said.

"You're not what I expected. You're younger and more genteel. You remind me," she said to the older woman, "of a Shaker side chair."

"Hmmm," Lucille Price Calvino said with a sly smile, "I take it that you mean I belong in an old farmhouse."

"I can't believe that I just said that... a Shaker side chair. Well ok... Let me try to wiggle out of that silly comparison. You're made of solid cherry wood, extremely well constructed, unadorned - as in not gilding the lily... and made to last for the ages."

"Good Lord! If you put me on an auction block I'd bid on me."

Beryl laughed. "You wouldn't win."

They were still grinning when the waitress came to take their order. "Whatever this lady is having," Beryl said, "I'll have the same. She's doing something that I need to copy." Lucille Calvino ordered a cheese and lettuce sandwich which the waitress duplicated for Beryl.

The two women sat and faced each other, each wondering what the other knew about the extraordinary situation the will had created. Lucille Calvino had the disposition and appearance of being Beryl's older sister rather than her senior by thirty years. They spoke as familiars in a gossipy tone.

"I told you on the phone that I was writing a biography," Beryl confided, "but actually I'm a private investigator, hired by Martin Mazzavini. I met your son yesterday and explained my purpose here. Martin's grandfather has been having some very suspicious accidents."

"So I've heard," Lucille replied. "My son took me for a walk this morning. I'm so glad you're on the case. And he explained about the bug in his office. It is unbelievable. These people have always been odd, but this recent turn of events beggars description. What questions can I answer for you?"

"I'd like to know about Paolo's Aviation Week subscription... his Geologic Survey maps... his injuries and treatment in Canada... his subsequent depression... and then the reading of the will and your trip to Mexico. Let's start with aviation. What was his interest in supersonic transports?"

"I could tell that something was going on about the Concorde and there was another aircraft, too. I forget what it was called. He was interested in that, too. I could tell by his reaction to the evening news whenever the topic came up. He'd stop talking and hold up his hand to keep others from talking; and he'd listen to the news about the SST's."

"I think the other one was the Boeing 2707."

"Yes.. That's what it was called. 2707. I often heard him mention the Concorde and the 2707, but he never told me anything specific about them. As far as I knew it was just a means to an end for Paolo. He wanted to become a farmer or rancher in the Southwest. He wanted to grow oil beans but he needed money to build a farm house and to buy tractors and horses and dig a well. I don't know what all. That was his dream. Working on this SST project - whatever it was - was going to compensate him... at least that's what he thought. I had my hands full with the baby and trying to get by on the salary Antonio paid him. We had a teenage boy. You'd have to know the expenses involved in raising a teenaged boy to understand."

"Oh, believe me... I know. My son Jack is now in engineering school... in Arizona. He wants to get a PhD in engineering. I'm a widow, but I should have married somebody named Getty or Walton."

"Then you know how involved you get with your children. My husband's problems had to do with his family... always it was his family. He had dreams of taking us away from them, but he had no education. I think that's what becoming a bean farmer meant to him. He didn't need a degree to grow beans. The SST project - whatever it was - was beyond his scope. His family considered him a stupid weakling. He was neither and yet... yet he craved their approval."

"Did you ever hear him on the phone... talking to Lorenzo, for example, about the planes?"

"They had private ways to communicate. I remember thinking it was about the airplanes. I also remember that Paolo got Ronny a model Concorde."

"What happened with his injuries?"

"That is a very painful subject for me. My son knows nothing about it in any detail. I know you're not writing a book, but it's something that I think I ought to avoid discussing."

"Then that is the one thing I need to discuss. Something happened to Paolo that his father and his brother Giovanni punished him for. Giovanni clearly had a guilty conscience about it. Why else would he cut everyone else out of his will? He was atoning for something, and I need to know what that was. How was Paolo injured? There are expenses he incurred in April of 1971."

Lucille sighed. "It's so long ago... and I've spent years trying to purge it from memory. Sometimes when I think back about it, it seems so incomprehensible. I didn't understand it then and I don't understand it now. Only now, I've forgotten many of the details. But what I do remember, I'll tell you *confidentially*, since you think it will help.

"It began on a Good Friday. Paolo said that Lorenzo was trying to get us an invitation to his father's house for Easter dinner. That was always a big fiesta type affair in the Calvino family. Antonio's wife was very religious and so was Giovanni's wife. I don't think Lorenzo was religious about anything but jewelry. At any rate, it was an enormous holiday and Lorenzo led Paolo to believe that the family had taken to heart some speech or other that Pope Paul the Sixth had made about

Christian charity towards children, and in response, they were finally going to accept us. We figured that Stephanie - who was an adorable little girl - had softened their hearts. It was still cold. Easter fell in March but I got new Easter outfits for the kids and me. Paolo was so happy.

"But then just as we got home from Church... the kids and I went to a Methodist Church. Paolo went to Saint Mark's Catholic Church, but because he was living with me and we had not been married in the Church, he couldn't receive Communion. Anyway, he got a call asking him to come early for some kind of meeting before dinner. He just said that he'd be back to get us after the meeting. But he never came back. I didn't want to call them, so I waited. But when it started to get dark and he still wasn't home, I called Lorenzo. There was no answer. Then I called Antonio's house. It turned out that there was no dinner at Antonio's house. It was at Giovanni's house. I remember being stunned that they could lie about something so trivial. So I called Giovanni, and he said that Paolo never got there and that there had to be some mistake. He said, and these were his exact words, 'My dinner table seats twelve. My wife and me and our son. My parents. My brother and his wife and their five children. You can do arithmetic. Add it up.' And he hung up the telephone.

"I finally got through to Lorenzo and he acted surprised that I didn't know where Paolo was. He said that Paolo was furious when he found out that the kids and I were not invited to the dinner and to calm him down he drove him for miles along the Lake. He said they stopped in a tavern for a drink, but it didn't help. Paolo was still so irrational. Obviously he needed a rest. He wanted to bring him home, but Paolo said that he didn't want to ride with Lorenzo any more, and he demanded that he be let out of the car outside an inn. Lorenzo said that he told him to spend the night or however long it took to calm down, and if he cooled down enough and wanted Lorenzo to drive back and get him, he would. Lorenzo didn't want to make things worse. He said that the last thing he said to him was, 'Be sure to call Lucille so she doesn't worry.' But Paolo didn't call.

"Lorenzo warned me not to call the police since Calvino Investments would be harmed by a scandal. He said that there already was a rumor that Paolo was seeing another woman and that we were having some kind of 'open' marriage. 'Swingers' was the big sexual revolution - free love - at the time. I could hear the lie in his voice. The Calvinos never approved of me, but I know that they never stooped that low to say such a thing. I didn't believe that excuse for a minute. I called Lorenzo every day. He was getting frantic, I could tell. Then he said he had a lead and to give him a little more time to locate Paolo. He sent me money... as if it were Paolo's paycheck. I wanted to report Paolo missing. But he begged me not to and said that if I did Paolo would lose his job and any chance of being reunited with the family. Lorenzo was so emphatic about it. 'Do not involve the police!' That's what he said."

"When did Paolo get back?"

"Eight days later. He came home looking gaunt... he had lost weight. I was shocked at his appearance. *But his spirits were good!* In a way, he seemed proud of himself. I couldn't understand it. And then he showed me his injuries... Ah, I don't want to talk about it."

"Please, Mrs. Calvino. It is very important. The injuries took you to Canada. But why there? What happened to him?"

Lucille Calvino stirred her tea and stared out the window. Beryl did not try to hurry her. She waited without expression until Lucille decided to speak. "I suppose there's no way around it," she said, still looking out the window. Then she turned to Beryl. "But I definitely do not want my children to know any of this. Can you leave this information out of your reports?"

"Yes. I'm here to protect Massimiliano Mazzavini. Four attempts have been made on his life. Let me be clear. Lorenzo wants to overturn the new will, and to do that he will have to prove that you or your children told Giovanni lies about Lorenzo and influenced him to disinherit Lorenzo and his family. He fears that Mr. Mazzavini knows the truth of why Giovanni was so guilt-ridden about what he had done to Paolo. This is why Mazzavini's life is in such danger. They need to silence him.

Nobody's interested in publicity of any kind. That's why the attempts on his life are not a police matter."

"Then I'll just say it and trust to your discretion. A person or persons - I think that's how it is put - tried to force my husband to reveal information that they thought he possessed. I do not know what that information was. He never told me. But he did suffer terribly at their hands. He wasn't badly marked up... not in areas that you would normally see. His face, for example, was not marked. Yes, it bore the signs of strain. But his fingernails were all intact and he had no broken ribs or dislocated joints. But they did use electric shocks to his genitals. In fact, his scrotum was so badly burned, he had to be castrated."

Beryl gulped. "*Good grief!* What? And you don't know what it was? And Ronald doesn't know?"

"No. None of it."

"Lorenzo had to have known! That had to be the five thousand dollar expenditure for which there are no receipts. My God!"

"He gave us five thousand. That was enough in those days. Paolo was in the hospital for a few days. We stayed at a motel in Ottawa. He told the doctors that he was shocked on his genitals in a terrible accident. While he was naked he bumped into some live wires. Some such story. Since the rest of his body was unmarked, they believed him, I suppose. So that he wouldn't become effeminate they prescribed testosterone and I think that had a negative effect on him."

"But you say that despite the torture, his spirits were high. I don't understand."

"I don't either. But he wouldn't explain anything. It was for my protection, he said."

"When did he start to get depressed... suicidally so?"

"I recall that for Memorial Day he had expected to be invited to a family picnic. I told him there would be no invitation, but he had hoped so much." She sighed. "He was such a fool when it came to his family. Of course, we were not invited. And then he was certain we'd be invited to a Fourth of July picnic. I thought his desperation was becoming pathological. His hopes were insane. But I couldn't keep looking for ways to excuse them. He was so moody and volatile. I tried to tell him that in ten years it would all be forgotten and that when we had our bean farm we'd be fine. Naturally, we weren't invited to any July Fourth picnic. He started to go downhill after that. August was bad... but September he was living in terror. He was acting paranoid. He'd walk Ronny to school. He'd check under the car before he started it. It was terrible. We had to leave the lights off at night. He got a dog from the pound. He was terrified of something, but he would never tell me what it was."

"Did you discuss his problem with the doctor who prescribed the testosterone?"

"Yes. He was getting shots from a local doctor. Paolo insisted that I not call that doctor. So I called the doctor in Canada and told him how volatile Paolo's moods were. He asked me to drive up there with him. But Paolo wouldn't go. He started to get along with his family a little better. In fact Lorenzo became kinder to him and talked to me about getting Paolo a place in a rest facility. He said not to consider it a sanitarium, but just a place where executives go to unwind and talk things over with a doctor. Paolo thought that Lorenzo's offer was proof that he was getting back into the family's good graces. And then Antonio died."

"How did Paolo react to the news?"

"By then his emotions were up, down, on, off. He had been assured that Antonio had divided the estate between the three of them - the three sons. Giovanni, Lorenzo, and Paolo were going to run the business. Lorenzo said that he'd 'take him under his wing.' They joked about the money Paolo would inherit... that he could finally buy some Italian suits and shoes - that was always a joke they had. By then he had stopped hoping to be a bean farmer. But after the will was read, and he had been disinherited, we simply couldn't stay in the same city or even country with the others."

"Did you talk to Lorenzo?"

"He said he didn't know what was going on. He thought Paolo had gone to Ottawa for a medical problem but he didn't know what it was. He didn't know what kind of medication Paolo was on, but maybe it was having a bad effect on him. Maybe Paolo had said something nasty to his father. Nobody called it "Roid Rage" in those days, but people who took testosterone apparently did have personality changes. He wanted me to take Paolo to see another doctor, but Paolo refused. Instead, we went to Mexico. I thought the change would do him good."

"Any specific reason why you picked Mexico."

"It was cheaper to live there. My daughter was a toddler. My son a teenager. My husband was a psychological wreck, and I had to take care of him and the baby. His mother had given him money... secretly... and we could live on it in Mexico. And naturally, we wanted to get as far away from Chicago as we could. So when some people he knew told him about an archeological dig way down near Tehuantepec, he wanted to go and I told him that I, too, wanted to live down there. Paolo always liked mesoamerican art. Indian art fascinated him. The wind was terrible. I remember that."

"Tell me about the actual suicide. Did he leave a note?"

"He left two pieces of paper. He wrote a poem on one, and on the other he wrote, 'Lucille - you, Ronny, and Steffi are my North, East, and South. I will follow the Lord of Light into my West.' He also liked Zen Buddhism and often talked about someone who came from the West."

"Bodhidharma," Beryl said.

"Yes... that sounds right. Bodhidharma, who discovered Zen."

"In a manner of speaking. What was the poem about?"

"I never got to read it properly. I got up in the morning and when he wasn't there, I thought he had gone to the beach... he was quite a beach comber. I didn't know he was dead. He had gotten up before dawn and loaded his pockets with heavy stones. I think he also had some in a net bag that he tied to his belt. He just walked into the ocean. I got up and made breakfast and was bathing Steffi when someone came running to the house. His body had been found on the beach. His shirt was torn off and the net bag had broken but was still attached to his belt. He had been flung against a jetty and was tangled in kelp. I thought that perhaps he had been bitten by a shark. The police came to get his papers. I was hysterical and it was then that I saw the suicide notes. I saw the poem only briefly. I was crying and could barely see the words, let alone read them. It described how he had been tortured and humiliated by the Army when they were trying to force him to say or do something. But since they were unable to break him, he died a heroic death. Something like that... It made no sense and I could barely read the writing."

"The *Army?* He was a civilian. For some reason I suspected that it was a Mafia type of torture. But, *wow!* The army? I confess... I didn't see that coming. Or, do you think it was a mental illness... an hallucination of some sort?"

"He didn't seem deranged at all. But that Army torture business... maybe that's why the police kept the poem. It had political value... anti-American, I guess. At any rate, they said they lost the poem in the shuffle. I'd give anything to have that poem in my hands again. I once went to a hypnotist to see if I could recall the lines under hypnosis. But I couldn't be hypnotized. I was lucky to get back his passport. I paid extra to have him buried down there. Because he was a suicide they didn't want him to be buried in a Catholic cemetery. Someone told the priest that he had drowned accidentally. So they put his grave in a corner plot... close to the road. And for the sake of his soul I put a veil over my head and went to Mass. I don't think I could take more controversy. I came home to live with my parents. What was the point of bringing him back?"

"If you should remember anything more about the poem or any other detail, let me know. It could be important."

After being admitted to the Illinois Bar, Martin Mazzavini spent his first year sitting behind his desk, looking handsome, prosperous, and smart... the kind of young attorney who had a position with a prestigious law firm that had corporate clients who allowed him to pay thousands for a suit and hundreds for a tie. In reality, he avoided the practice of corporate law as much as it, apparently, avoided him. He had won a major criminal case in Arizona and his grandfather encouraged him to focus on criminal law. Violent crimes were becoming more common among corporate executives. It was good for the firm to have a criminal lawyer on staff for whenever a corporate client was named a defendant.

His was still mopping-up after his big Arizona win; but he was anxious to get involved in a new case and to continue to develop his reputation as a tough defense attorney. He was still in the "anxious to become" phase when, on Thursday afternoon, he played solitaire on his iPad as he waited for Beryl to return from her brunch with Lucille Calvino. He had spent the morning gathering intel on the Mafia's activities in 1970 and 1971 and had come up with a few interesting cases.

Beryl, dressed now in normal street clothing, checked in with the receptionist and was immediately directed back to Martin's office. She pushed open the glass door and looked around the room. "This definitely is not you."

"What then?" he asked. "Wagon wheels, a saddle... some spurs hanging on the wall. The goddamned door is glass so I can't nail a horseshoe over it. It's chrome and glass and leather and wall-to-wall carpeting, and it looks like every other high priced attorney's office in the western hemisphere. Is that what you're trying to tell me? That it's not me because - what's that line by Oscar Wilde? *Be yourself! Everybody else is taken.*"

"An Italian esthete? You're now an Italian esthete? I'm shocked. And no, I don't see you as western, either. But let's get one very important thing accomplished before we start with the little things. Would you be a sweet boy and ask your secretary to make an appointment for me with her hairdresser Saturday. I must get my hair done for the party. Use all your muscle to get it done."

"Yes, Ma'am," he said, and he immediately buzzed his secretary. "My Grandfather's biographer needs to have her hair done for his party Saturday night. Could you use your considerable influence to get her an appointment? Tell them to bill the firm."

Within ten minutes, Beryl had an appointment. "Now that we have the important business out of the way," she teased Martin, "we can discuss other matters. Turn on some music."

Martin put a disk of Mahler's 5th Symphony into the CD slot of his radio and put his phone and iPad in a desk drawer. Then he guided

Beryl to the black leather couch and whispered, "What did you learn from Lucille Calvino? Tell me about her."

"She's a plain but attractive woman. I liked her. I probably could have talked to her all day... about anything. It was difficult for me to imagine that Paolo could have killed himself and left her behind to face the music alone... with two kids." She got out her little blue notebook. "I made a note to ask you to look into the insurance situation. He may have figured that treating his mental state would have been so expensive that any insurance money - assuming he had any - would have been consumed by his medical expenses. So he killed himself and left her with money. This is a frequent occurrence in suicides. His mother also gave him money on the QT. See what you can find out about that. What made his mom the only Calvino who cared about his welfare? Maybe it was mother love. Maybe something more.

"Now... the news. Before they went to Ottawa for treatment, Paolo had been held for eight days by a person or persons unknown who had harmed him. He had evidently been tortured in a way that didn't show on the outside." She held her index finger against his lips. "This cannot go past this moment. I'll tell you and then we'll both forget it. Agreed?"

"Give me a dollar and I'll lose my license if I reveal it."

Beryl was startled. "I'm your agent!"

"I don't care. I want the additional protection."

Beryl sighed and took a dollar from her purse. She put it into his hand. "We are now attorney and client, right?"

"Yes. Anything you tell me is absolutely confidential."

She bent over and whispered in his ear, "Electric prods had been used on his scrotum which caused such severe burns that he had to be castrated. That's why they went to Ottawa for medical treatment."

"*Christ!* Nobody knows that! Nobody even *suspects* that! My God! Now you see what I'm so worried about. These people are dangerous. Jesus!"

Beryl told him about the "directional" suicide note and the poem he had written that the police had taken. "But here is the real kick in the ass," she said. "Lucille didn't have a chance to study the poem... she read it quickly and through tearful eyes; but she says that the poem described how Paolo had been tortured by the Army when they tried to get him to reveal some information; but he did not break and tell them what they wanted, and so he died a hero's death."

"The Army? The U.S. Army?"

"I don't see how it could have been any other army. He never went anywhere."

"Could he have meant the C.I.A.?"

"Inside the U.S.? They don't function inside the U.S."

"Maybe he just *thought* they were army. He had never been in the service. How would he be able to tell a real soldier from a fake one? And for that matter, the Mafia uses terms like Lieutenant and soldier."

"Good point." Beryl made a note in her little blue book.

"The Army?" Martin remained incredulous. "What did he mean by 'Army'?"

"The only military connection I can make is with that supersonic transport business. We think of it as just a passenger plane, but there were military aspects to these planes and certainly to supersonic aircraft in general. Paolo was interested enough in the Concorde to give his son a model of one to construct. Ronald says that model making was not his hobby or anyone else's. So this was something special. All through the 1960's there was constant talk about the Concorde and Boeing's 2707 and the Russian version. The military significance can't be overlooked."

"From what I learned about the SST situation," Martin countered, "the problem had nothing to do with the military. Before the Concorde ever landed on U.S. soil, there were major objections to the noise. New York banned them and then when it was allowed to land, it could land only in Washington, D.C. But then everybody raved about it so much that New York reconsidered and wanted the Concorde to be able to land. This was a major turning point. The developers began to seek new solutions. They started to push the AST instead of the SST. Lockheed and Boeing took another look at "Advanced Supersonic Transport" - and in 1970 new life was breathed into the program. If New York could reconsider, other major U.S. cities were going to give the problem another look. They couldn't stop the sonic booms but they could put them outside city limits."

"So the AST, aside from technical changes to the aircraft, mandated terminals that were not in major cities, but near them. Then," Beryl reasoned, "that has to be what the big investment was going to be... land for terminals near the big cities that the supersonic planes would serve."

"That has to be it," Martin concurred. "This might also mean that there would be federal grants to build new terminals instead of just enlarging existing runways and terminal facilities. But I still don't see how Paolo Calvino could figure in all this."

"Then that has to be what those Geologic Survey maps were for," Beryl concluded. All the money that Lorenzo lost could have been in land speculation. But what could Paolo possibly know that he refused to tell the people who tortured him?" Beryl asked. "Maybe he didn't know what they wanted him to tell them. No! Wait! Since he was so upbeat and sort of proud of himself - as Lucille says - maybe he knew something and held out under all that pressure."

"What could he have known? As I read the signs on Memory Lane, during that period governments all over the world wanted a Concorde terminal. Citizens didn't want any part of them. Farmers said the chickens wouldn't lay eggs and the cows wouldn't give milk and fisherman said the fish were scared off. But all that was known during the 1960s. Those SST airports had every indication of being built and the noise was just something that rural folks would have to get used to. The terminals were still hot prospects in the Spring of 1971."

"We're forgetting the big aviation news of the time. Boeing introduced the 747. And that is what probably put the kebosh on those terminals. The SST just wasn't cost effective. But, of course, it wasn't all that 'cost effective' before. The rich and important folks in New York and Washington continued to fly in the Concorde.

Martin looked up. "I made a note: on September 4th, 1971, the U.S. cancelled Boeing's 2707 SST. I guess that's when the handwriting was on the wall for the terminals. If the U.S. wasn't going to produce an SST aircraft, that had to kill the 'nearby city' talk." He considered the questions. "So in April of 1971 people still thought the Concorde was 'coming to a neighborhood near you' kind of thing? And what Paolo knew was the list of intended airport sites near the other cities where the Concorde would land." He gestured frustration with both hands. "But what could he possibly know that they would torture him for? Army or Mafia or KGB? Paolo was a clerk! Decisions about SST airports don't come his way. This is insane!"

"Make a note in your little blue book. But first think about this question: what is there about it that would cause someone to want to harm Massimiliano Mazzavini forty years later?"

"Jesus! This is so crazy! Why did Antonio cut Paolo out of his will in 1971 and why did Giovanni Calvino dump Lorenzo and bestow his fortune on Paolo's family in 2011? Does Lucille know anything at all about why Giovanni gave everything to Paolo's family?"

"She doesn't have a clue. Let's move on. How did you make out with your Mafia or other financial disaster research in that time period?"

"Floppy discs were invented. What the hell are floppy discs? NASA was on the moon. Kent State. Rubrik's Cube. Aswan Dam. VCR tape. Nixon was president and there was Ping Pong diplomacy. I got a list of important events, but aside from the European Common Market, not much happened financially on a global basis. Locally, in 1971 people lost money in land deals, but in actual land speculation, only an unnamed consortium of local investors apparently took a bath. I asked my father about it. He called a few people and said that the consortium was actually one of the Mafia families, but he couldn't find out which one. He guessed that it was the Nievo family."

"Are any of the family members still alive? I don't want to hazard a guess about Mafia life expectancy."

Martin laughed. "These families don't have genes and chromosomes to worry about. And no grandfathers... Godfathers, yes. Grandfathers, no. Two men who had been associated with the big families were sentenced to Joliet for life without parole... for an unrelated crime that occurred in the 80's. Some cops were killed in a shootout about some gambling syndicate beef. They were transferred to Stateville Prison here in Chicago when Joliet was closed around ten years ago. The feds pretty much broke up the original Mafia families. All we're likely to find are these "army" types... lieutenants and soldiers."

"Let's go talk to them. Maybe they know something about 'the army members' or whoever it was that got Lorenzo into forty million dollars worth of debt."

"Unfortunately, one died last summer and the other one declines all interviews. Parini, his name is. Alfredo Parini. He might have been a lieutenant in the Greco family. Lorenzo's wife was Greco's daughter. Parini gave an interview once and talked too much. Now he talks to no one. Since he's exhausted all his appeals, he doesn't even get to see young handsome criminal lawyers."

"You already asked?"

"I didn't think it would hurt to inquire."

"It would be great if we could talk to him. And is there no file anywhere about the specifics of what Lorenzo paid off with all that money from Giovanni? No receipts of any kind?"

"For all those millions there are probably many files... but they are all in Lorenzo's keeping. And no matter how nicely we ask him, I doubt that he'll let us see the records.... unless..."

"Unless what?" she asked.

"You're still so fetching in your drug store sunglasses. Maybe you can wink at him and he'll spill his guts." Martin tried and failed to sound serious. He was grinning as he turned his face away.

"*Nobody likes you very much.* Isn't it time we went to get your grandfather?"

Martin Mazzavini ate his pizza sitting across the table from Beryl. She hadn't told him about her plans and he didn't like to learn about them as a witness to their execution. As she got out her cellphone and called her office in Philadelphia, Martin observed with a slight feeling of rejection.

In Philadelphia, George and Sensei had finished cleaning the office. "Let's see what Beryl's got in the freezer that we can nuke," George said.

"I don't feel like going to a restaurant and I'm not going to risk driving home in snow only to come back to attend services."

"You have some clothes in my apartment in case you need them," Sensei offered.

"I've got plenty of stuff here. I think I have more clothing here than I have at home. She irons my shirts."

"Everything I have is wash and wear. But I never have to dress in business clothing."

"I ought to become a monk. Christ knows I live like one. I live more like a monk than you do and you are one."

"No.. I am a priest. There's a difference."

As they climbed the enclosed staircase that led to Beryl's second storey apartment, they could hear the office phone extension ring in her office-bedroom. George hurriedly opened her door and rushed a few steps forward to answer the phone.

Beryl wasted no time with pleasantries. "Do you know any retired FBI agent or someone high in the police department who might know how to induce a prisoner in Stateville prison to grant me - the famous biographer of Mazzavini and Calvino - an interview? The inmate is an old mafioso who doesn't accept invitations for interviews."

"Let me think..." George thought and then decided he needed to ask someone else to think. "I'll have to get back to you on that. How's the case?"

"Getting tricky. The big birthday party for Mazzavini is Saturday night. I'll be seeing a hair stylist. Any color you want me to do my hair?"

"I liked it when you did it that grey-blonde color. It needs cutting, too. I've been meaning to tell you that."

"Shut up and put Sensei on the phone. You're giving me heartburn. Are the two of you raiding my freezer?"

"Naturally. It's snowing here. Percy just helped me to sweep and mop the office floor. I'm going to services tonight. I'll be doin' *your* job of ringing the little bell. The workload is so great I'm also spending the night in Jack's room. As for Percy's sermon tonight... I don't know what he's going to expound on... what sin is the sin of the week... so don't ask.

Here, you can talk to Percy yourself. I just remembered somebody I can ask about the FBI in Chicago." He held the phone away from his mouth. "Percy! Beryl's on the phone. She wants to consult with you about hair color."

Sensei Percy Wong, the head and only priest of the small Zen temple down the street from Wagner & Tilson's office, answered to "Percy" when George called him and, because he was Beryl's karate teacher as well as her Buddhist priest, he answered to Sensei when she called him. He answered the phone, "The timer is set to go off shortly. Ash Blonde. What else?"

"I'm going down to the south of Mexico... on the Pacific side. It's rebel country and I can't bring weapons into Mexico. Can you go?"

"Sure. I'll be your backup. When? And for how long?"

"I'd be leaving here on Sunday and be back on Wednesday."

"You'd want to meet me in Mexico City on Sunday?"

"Yes.. We'd have to take a smaller flight to Juchitan or Oaxaca on Monday morning and then rent a car. We can decide when we rendezvous in Mexico City. George is going to let me know if he found a contact for me here in the prison. I'll call you back tomorrow. Are you two going out to play shuffleboard after services tomorrow night?"

"Probably. It's snowing now, but if the weather holds we'll be playing at the *Four Kegs*."

"OK... I'll call you tomorrow afternoon." She heard the microwave bell. "Go eat your dinner and tell George to call with the information. If he talks to the contact, tell him the cover will be that I'm writing a biography about the Calvino family... and want to hear the prisoner's side of the story. Say that I have a hunch that in regards to that Paolo mess years ago, the others are trying to load the guilt onto him. I want to give him a chance to tell his side and redeem his reputation with his friends and enemies."

"Wait a sec..." Sensei relayed the message to George. Beryl could hear George yell, "Good idea. Ok I'll run with it and let her know."

"All right," Beryl called. "I'll talk to you later." She clicked off her phone.

Mazzavini was subdued. "You're going to Mexico without me?"

"Of course. It's rebel country... dangerous. You're paying me to take the risks. I can't justify risking your life. Things are dangerous enough right here; and you need to look after your grandfather. All I want to do is to verify an old death certificate and to see if an old file contains a bizarre poem. We need to be sure of the manner in which Paolo died. And we need that damned poem."

"I just thought that since we were working together...."

"My God! You're pouting!"

"No, I'm not! I just wanted to go, that's all."

"I'll talk to Sensei and see what he thinks."

"Good. He'll say 'yes.' He likes me."

"I know he likes you. You're the reason he met Miss Lee, the great love of his life. He may try to adopt you."

"I'll anticipate his approval and make hotel reservations in Mexico City for Sunday night. Do we register as Mr. and Mrs?"

"No. Doctor and Patient or Mother and Son. Take your pick. Actually, get a double room for you and Sensei and a single for me."

George Wagner called back an hour later. He had called the friend of a friend of the warden and succeeded in getting the warden to ask the inmate, one Alfredo Parini, if he wanted to talk to a woman who was writing a biography of Calvino and Mazzavini. The warden didn't think he'd agree, but he supposed that Parini felt more free to talk now that the other mafioso member had died. He suggested to Parini that maybe the other guy had tried to implicate him in other crimes and Parini said, "They're still trying to dump on me, but I've had enough shit put on my head. Sure, I'll talk to... 'the biographer.'"

"That," George said, "is the good news. The bad news is that you have to be at the prison no later than 10 a.m. tomorrow morning. And the interview will take place in the warden's office. Parini made the warden agree to that so that Parini wouldn't be misquoted."

"That's good news," Beryl said. "I'll work up my questions this afternoon and evening. Maybe we'll finally get somewhere. And tell

Sensei that Martin and I will meet him in Mexico City Sunday. We'll go to Tehuantepec Monday morning. Martin will call Sensei with airline and hotel details. Martin will make the reservations and the firm here will pay for all travel expenses."

She put her phone away. "Now all that we need to do is to get more information about the forty million dollars that was lost back in 1971. Your grandfather won't tell us anything, but maybe your grandmother remembers something of value."

They drove out to the Mazzavani estate, which was a curiously isolated place, Beryl thought. She had imagined that the famous lawyer would live in an enclave of the rich. But he did not. Instead he had a house and grounds that more resembled a Kentucky horse breeders estate with its whitewashed "Warm Barn" horizontal log fencing and its brick colonial style dwellings - the main house, the garage, and a guest house. Hedges lined the driveway and Rhododendron bushes flanked the buildings.

"It's kind of homey," Beryl said. "Unpretentious. I like it."

"This is where I was raised as a kid.... when I was raised at all. My father's house is not unpretentious. Fortunately, I spent more time with my grandparents, especially with my Nana."

Nana Mazzavini insisted that they have dinner, but Martin declined because he didn't want to include his grandfather in the conversation. The senior Mazzavini was napping and Martin quickly got his grandmother into the living room to ask what she remembered about land dealings in the 1970-71 period.

"Oh, my goodness!" she exclaimed. "That is a long time ago. Does this have anything to do with Lorenzo Calvino's big loss in the real estate market? I don't think I'm supposed to talk about it but what do you want to know?"

"What real estate investments did he make?" Martin tried to sound causal.

"Well, you know I never could abide him," she turned to Beryl, "or the woman he married. You know how you always count the silver after you give a dinner party... because you're afraid that a piece of flatware could have been thrown out when the plates were scraped? Well, when the two of them ate at your table, you wanted to count the silver to see how many pieces they made off with. They just inspired fear of themselves... fear that they were going to get you to invest in a bad stock or something... deliberately make you lose money to cover their own losses. Lorenzo and his wife. Two peas in a pod. She was one of those trophy wives - all flash except when it came to brains. That woman was just plain stupid. They made a good pair. Stupid and Evil. Her father was one of those Italian criminals."

"Gee, Nana, could you give me an example of how stupid and evil they were."

"Their evil was greed and just plain old bad taste. I don't mean just their vulgarity in things - you know, furniture, clothing, jewelry; but it was the way they spoke to people. They were cruel to servants and insulting to anyone they thought was a social inferior. And the funny thing was that after awhile it became something to talk about, as if folks were having a "can you top this" contest about the most outrageously nasty remarks they made. After awhile, as I've said, people just built up an immunity to them and everything they said was a source of amusement. Lorenzo always looked like one of those... I can't remember the name... but they are men who wear a lot of gold jewelry around their neck and sit at bars waiting to pick up or be picked up... I can't remember which... and I forget what they're called."

"Gigolo?" offered Martin.

"No... something else."

"Beryl said he sounded like a 'Lounge lizard.'"

"Yes!" Nana exclaimed. "That's it, exactly! That's what people said Lorenzo always looked like. A lounge lizard." She put her head back and laughed so hard that she had to put her finger on her upper denture so that it wouldn't come loose. "What do you want to know about him... Lorenzo the Lounge Lizard?"

"How did he lose so much money?" Martin asked. "And until Beryl used the term, I had never heard it before. And you two agree on it. Lounge Lizard. Somehow it fits."

Nana patted his hand. "You need to get out of the house more, Marty. You're such a handsome boy. But you spend too much time alone. Lorenzo's wife? I forget her name."

"It's Monica, Nana."

"Monica... Monica Greco Calvino, Mrs. Lorenzo Calvino. Thought she knew everything. The ladies at the beauty parlor used to laugh at her. She wore her hair in one of those shag haircuts. Bangs and straight down the sides and back like Jane Fonda. But Monica had no forehead. They said it was because she had no brain. She's the one who cost him so much money although, frankly, he approved of everything she did. He didn't trust anybody and she was the daughter of one of those unsavory people we honest Italians don't talk about."

"You've got me interested, Nana. What happened?"

"Well, he sent her to many places to buy up farm land... undeveloped land. I mean, they may have grown farming things on it, but they didn't have houses or factories on it."

"Undeveloped land."

"Yes... Plain land. She went to an area, wanting to buy land. And instead of placing herself in the hands of a reputable real estate agent and letting him do the thing he was trained to do, she, of course, knew better and thought she'd shop around for the best price. So she picked a few parcels of land in the area she was interested in, and then she called a bunch of real estate agents trying to see who could get her the best price. And each one of them approached the owners of the land and told them that he had a buyer if the owner wanted to sell. It didn't take long for each owner to think, 'My goodness! All these people want to buy my land!' And the owner would increase his asking price. He'd ask for more... and more! That's called the Law of Supply and Demand. That's exactly what the law is. The more people want something, the more you can charge them. This dumb bunny Monica kept trying to get a cheaper price by calling one agent after another; and each of those owners thought they were going to get very, very rich. The price went higher and higher. And Lorenzo knew all about it. Every night she'd call him and tell him what was going on. He thought he was competing against other land speculators! He had no idea he was competing against himself. So he borrowed a lot of money to buy the land. She was an executive of their corporation, and she also had Lorenzo's power of attorney. She signed the papers. So he owned an enormous amount of that undeveloped land. Actually, he had borrowed most of the money from his father-in-law. He told the old man how rich he was going to be; and the old man also borrowed money to lend to him and Monica."

"That was stupid. No wonder he lost money."

"But Marty, that wasn't the half of it. When her father found out how stupid Lorenzo and his daughter had been, he naturally gave most of the blame to Lorenzo and he made him pay back every penny he borrowed. Some people said he also charged him interest. I don't know if that's true or not."

Beryl and Martin Mazzavini look at each other incredulously. "So this," Beryl said, "is why Lorenzo had to come up with forty million. Amazing."

"Let's be sure about this," Martin cautioned, turning to his grandmother. "Nana, why did Lorenzo want the land?" Martin asked.

"Airports! He wanted to build airports! He had a close personal friend who had a close personal friend who worked in Washington, D.C. and knew the secret locations that the government had picked for the terminals for the SST airplanes. It seems so funny now because they are things that never happened. That Concorde doesn't even fly anymore. It's hard to imagine how excited everybody was when it first flew. It was like the chinchilla craze. People were going to become chinchilla millionaires. It's true. All they had to do was buy a breeding pair of chinchillas and let them do their mating thing and the owners would become millionaires in no time. Chinchillas breed fast and their pelts were supposed to be so valuable. I knew so many people who bought breeding pairs of chinchillas. But I never knew one person who made a nickel out of breeding chinchillas. Now... the Animal Abuse people won't even let folks wear fur.

"It was the same, I guess, with that Concorde." Everybody got so excited about it. They didn't know anything about aviation, but the excitement just carried them away. And since when did a lack of knowledge ever stop anyone from doing what they fantasized about?"

"What happened to the chinchillas?" Martin was amused. He had never heard about the chinchilla craze.

"They went to the same place as the Concorde went. To some big dream graveyard in the sky. The difference, as your grandfather likes to say, 'was one of degree not kind.' The same kind of inflated imagination was at work. It was just that they lost more money on the Concorde than they lost on those little animals. Imagine how Lorenzo felt when he learned that there wasn't going to be any landing sites in the U.S. outside of Washington, D.C. and New York City.

"He was stuck with all this property that was way-overpriced. He tried to blame his wife, which did not make Mr. Greco happy. He lent Lorenzo the money because Lorenzo assured him that his "inside source" knew for a certainty *that* those terminals would be built and *where* those terminals would be built. Greco suspected that Lorenzo and his friend were more than friends. That's what he said. I guess he figured that when he heard that Lorenzo was trying to blame Monica for the purchase of the land. But she saved Lorenzo's life. If she hadn't been Greco's daughter and the mother of Greco's grandchildren, Greco would have shot him dead - after he got his money back." She heard a noise and held her finger to her lips.

Massimiliano Mazzavini had come down the stairs. "What have we here?" he said to Beryl. She stood up and walked to him and he hugged her. "She's the one who saved Martin's life down in Arizona," he explained to his wife. "Give her anything she wants."

"We're here just to check up on you, Pop Pop," Martin said.

"It sounded to me as though you were going down Memory Lane."

"Ah, Mr. Mazzavini, we have no memories that don't include you." Beryl was not entirely sure of what her remark meant, but it was something to say at an awkward moment.

"Well, Pop Pop, it's great to see you walking around and looking so strong."

Beryl looked at her watch and indicated that it was time to go. "I look forward to dancing with the famous Massimiliano Mazzavini on Saturday night."

"And dance you shall," said the elderly man.

As they walked to the car, Martin said, "For your information, I know how to dance, too."

"Sure," she said, "When somebody's shootin' at your feet. Then you're a regular Fred Astaire."

"Do innocent bystanders a favor and don't bring your Beretta. I intend to be armed."

FRIDAY, JANUARY 6, 2012

While Martin waited outside the prison in his car, Beryl presented her card to the warden's secretary and was immediately shown into his office to conduct the interview. As was customary, she brought with her only a notepad and pencil.

Warden James had a guard stationed outside his office even though the inmate inside was nearly eighty years old and posed no threat to anyone.

When all the introductions had been made, Beryl said, "I'm interested in the Calvino - Mazzavini relationship. Massimiliano Mazzavini was a childhood friend of Giovanni Calvino, but he didn't become Calvino's attorney until 1971 at the time of the Paolo Calvino problem. The rumor," she said, although she did not know of any such rumor, "is that you oversaw that eight day..." she cleared her throat as she searched her mind for a sanitized way to say 'torture,' "attempt to persuade him to disclose certain information."

"Oh... about the SST landing sites."

Beryl smiled and thought, "This has to be too easy." She nodded. "Yes, the SST terminal sites."

"That's a whole lot of ancient history. It wasn't an operation I oversaw. I had nothin' to do with it. But I'm not surprised. After all these years they're still trying to finger me for every dirty job they did. They're embarrassed. What? Is the truth gonna' come out? Is somebody runnin' for Congress?"

"Just my book which I hope somebody will read in order to learn the truth."

Alfredo Parini put his hands behind his head as if a cop had ordered him to do so. He took a deep breath and thought for a long minute. "As I recall it... Greco, who was my boss, had one daughter, Monica, who was married to Lorenzo Calvino. Lorenzo had a friend who knew where all the SST terminals were gonna be built. They weren't gonna use the big inner-city airports because those were too noisy already and they didn't want the 'boom-boom' SST airplanes flyin' over them. So the government picked a town near the big city destination and that's where they were gonna build the terminals. Knowing which town - now, that information was worth a lot of money. A smart operator could buy up that land dirt-cheap and then make millions sellin' it to the government and the big airlines.

"Lorenzo and Monica talked Greco into lending them the money to buy up all the land around the towns that were chosen. I think there were nine or ten terminal sites. They were gonna make millions. They were competing against Howard Hughes and the big boys. As I said, Lorenzo knew a guy who knew a guy. It was stupid to trust this kind of information, but nobody ever accused Lorenzo of not being stupid.

People were already fed up with the noise of ordinary jets. They didn't want those SST's landing there, too. Those fast planes didn't carry many people and the thought was that when all the airlines converted to them there would be hundreds of those planes landing and taking off every day. People knew about the booms from the fighter planes that broke the sound barrier. Jesus! It shook your whole house!

"The trick was in knowin' which town had been picked." He laughed. "There's lotsa' little towns around a big city. I remember a few. For service to Philadelphia they would put the SST terminal in Wilmington, Delaware which is only about twenty-five miles away but had a great highway between. And Wilmington is closer to the Atlantic Ocean. Then Howard Hughes was supposed to be buying land north of Las Vegas for a big SST airport. Everybody wanted a piece of the action.

"I think Lorenzo and Monica bought a lot of land... in California... in Washington State... in Florida... in Texas. Yeah, it was outside Houston, Texas in a place called Texas City... near an oil refinery or something.

We're talking big money, here. Greco, my boss, gave them plenty - some that he even borrowed - just on Lorenzo's word that he knew as a sure thing which towns would be picked. So Greco's beef was with Lorenzo. He didn't care about Paolo. It was the Nievo family who tried to get Paolo to talk. And the guy you want to talk to - the inmate in this prison that is probably the source that people were leading you to - died last year. Ask the warden. Alonzo Ruggieri of the Nievo family. They wanted to know which terminal sites had been picked so that they would buy the right land. They already were buyin' land. They just wanted to be sure they were buyin' the right land. They're the ones who nailed Paolo. Not Greco."

"Why would they think Paolo knew?" Beryl asked. "Lorenzo never would have trusted such information to his little brother. Paolo had no money and as far as the family was concerned, he was an outsider."

"Paolo knew. Maybe he helped Lorenzo buy some of the land. I don't know. But he knew. Nievo's boys did everything they could to make Paolo talk, but he wouldn't tell them anything. He keeps repeatin' the names of the big cities... not the nearby town that's gonna' be the terminal site. And then after a week or so and he don't break, they find maps in Paolo's car which is parked outside Lorenzo's house. These maps that show the exact areas of the sites. Paolo says he don't know how these maps got in his car. They had what they wanted, so they let him go. He had a hood over his head the whole time. He didn't know who was puttin' the screws to him. Paolo was not a street guy. He didn't know squat. They took him down to Cabrini Green and dumped him on the sidewalk. Somebody put him in a cab and he went home to his wife."

"You're sure Paolo never told them anything?" Beryl asked

"I'm sure. I remember that. We all admired the guy for not breakin'. He took a lot of punishment but he never broke. We used to think Paolo was a pussy, but he was tough as nails. Some people said maybe Lorenzo gave him the wrong names, that he figured Paolo was a pussy and would give up the wrong names. Nievo's boys said that he was supposed to break easy. But Paolo didn't give up any names. When the maps were found in his car, Nievo believed that they were the names that he had tried to keep secret. All I know is that Greco lent his daughter and Lorenzo a lot of money and they bought land around those towns before anybody else could. And then the government cancelled all the SST plans and everybody who speculated in land for SST sites anywhere in the country got burned bad. Nievo. Greco. A lotta people lost big bucks."

"Were the names, in fact, the real sites that Lorenzo had bought?"

Warden James stood up. "I'm sorry," he said. "I made the time available to accommodate a friend. But now, I fear, I'm running too far behind schedule."

Beryl stood up and shook hands with him. "I think I have plenty to work with here." She thanked Parini and the warden and left the prison.

When Beryl got into the car and Martin asked how the interview went, she said, *"He was supposed to break easy."*

"What the hell does that mean?" Martin asked.

"I am totally confused. First, Parini says it was the Nievo family that abducted Paolo. He says that Paolo didn't ever know who had abducted him. We know that Parini worked for the Greco family. Lorenzo was married to Greco's daughter. So when Monica Greco Calvino bought that land with her husband, it was her father who lent him the money. Not any loan sharks. Lorenzo had to pay Greco back the money he lost. Maybe Greco threatened to do to Lorenzo what Nievo had done to Paolo."

"The Nievo family abducted Paolo?" Martin was incredulous. "How did they get involved?"

"Parini says it was the Nievo family. But I guess that anything is possible. I don't think it matters too much who it was... except... except for the maps turning up. At the end of Paolo's ordeal, somebody just happened to find maps in Paolo's car which was parked in front of Lorenzo's house, Parini said. But Paolo didn't know the maps were there. The maps showed the exact locations that Paolo wouldn't reveal.

"The questions then are, how did they know there were maps in the car, and what landing sites did the maps show? Were they the real ones Lorenzo bought? Or were they phony ones that Paolo had been led to believe were the landing sites so that when they tortured him, he'd break down and spout this misinformation... these phony sites. '*He was supposed to break easy.*' We don't even know if Paolo knew which sites Lorenzo and Monica bought."

"But if Paolo was *supposed* to break easy... that could mean that somebody counted on his breaking. Who but Lorenzo would profit from his breaking down and spreading misinformation? Christ! That's a horrible thought. I'm glad I'm an only child."

"The world would cease to spin if there were two of you on board," Beryl said, patting his head. "We have notes to make. Questions that need to be answered. Where was the land that Nievo invested in? And where was the land that Lorenzo invested in? There probably were no sites around Chicago. Coastal cities only, as far as I know. Get Houston on a map and see where Texas City, Texas, is located."

As Martin Googled up a map of Houston and Texas City just south of it, Beryl said, "A good way for us to fly back to Chicago from Tehuantepec is through Houston. Why don't we go look at the plat books around Texas City to see what we can find for land purchases. As to Paolo's ordeal, Parini told me that were it not for the inconvenience of Alonzo Ruggieri's death we could have learned everything we wanted to know about Paolo from him. Alonzo Ruggieri of the Nievo family was in prison the same time Parini was. He was also present during the torturing. Lord... but this is one Machiavellian deal."

"Welcome to the land of Gucci and Armani."

"The Medicis and Borgias would be more like it. And make a note to find out if Lorenzo used a special corporate name to buy the land. He would have had to file documents."

"I'll get on it, immediately.... as soon as we go have lunch and get back to my office. And then I'll ask my secretary to get the information for us. She loves this investigation stuff. So do I, but we have other things to do."

Martin called his secretary. "In 1971," he said, "Lorenzo Calvino formed a business entity of some kind... a partnership or a corporation... with his wife Monica Greco Calvino. I'd like you to stop whatever you're doing -" Beryl pretended to be filing her nails. Martin grabbed her fingers and put them in his mouth pretending to bite them. "I said... find out the name he used for that entity. Oh... and find out what you can about Alonzo Ruggieri who died in Stateville Prison last year. And get back to me as soon as possible."

At lunch, Martin asked, "What more do we have to do today?"

"I can't think. Frankly, I'm bushed. And tomorrow I'll be all day at the beauty parlor. There's the party tomorrow night; and then Sunday we fly to Mexico?"

Martin confessed to being tired, too. "I think it's the frustration. I'm getting so goddamned sick and tired of turning over a rock and finding another sidewinder."

Beryl laughed. "I know how you feel. Chicago is so full of sidewinders. The monotony of it all. One sidewinder after another. By the way, have you ever actually seen a sidewinder?"

Martin swatted her head. *"I'll tell you but you've got to ask me nicely."*

They returned to Martin Mazzavini's office and learned that Ruggieri's widow lived in town. They got her phone number and address. And the name of the corporation that Lorenzo had established was the *Calgrec Development Corporation.*

"Jesus," Martin said. "The idiot called his company the CDC."

They laughed about the name and decided to go back to Martin's apartment to watch a few movies and order pizza for dinner. Enough was enough.

As they watched *Dead Man,* Martin's phone rang. He looked at the caller I.D., switched the phone off, and resumed watching the movie. "Claudia," he said. "I told her to keep the ring. It was a gift, a token of my esteem. I hoped she would enjoy it. We were never engaged. I never asked her to marry me. I owe her no explanation."

"So your mind is no longer confused."

"That's right. I received confirmation from the *I Ching.*"

Beryl shook her head. "Rewind the movie a little," she said. "I missed some of the dialog."

SATURDAY, JANUARY 7, 2012

Downstairs in the ballroom, the orchestra was playing *Red Roses for a Blue Lady* as Martin and Beryl walked across the lobby to the coat check counter. Martin, formally attired down to his patent leather shoes, removed his Chesterfield as Beryl studied him in his unaccustomed garb. "Did you remember to take all the tags off?" she asked.

The question made him laugh as he removed the wrap from her shoulders and handed both outer garments to the clerk. "When we dance," he whispered as he guided Beryl to the staircase that led down into the ballroom, "I intend to step on your toes."

Beryl, resplendent in the black silk, silver-bead trimmed sari that Sensei had bought for her in Suriname, stood beside Martin at the top of the staircase. He was determined that everyone in the room should look up at her with admiration before he held out his left hand, palm down, for her to rest her right hand on. Together, smiling benignly at the upturned faces of the guests, they gracefully descended the stairs. "If you step on my toes I will consider it an assault, and I will defend myself," she whispered between smiling acknowledgements of the people who watched.

"Using one of your ka-ra-te moves? I don't think so."

"Think?" she asked. "You suppose... or guess? Do it and find out." The orchestra began to play *Stardust* as they reached the floor.

Massimiliano Mazzavini had walked across the room to greet them. He kissed Beryl's hand and with a sweeping gesture showed them to the table at which Martin's grandmother, father and mother sat. Beryl was surprised when he introduced her as his biographer to the little group of close relatives. Not even they, apparently, were allowed to know that she was investigating the near fatal accidents.

As Martin stood behind her, carefully pushing in her chair as she sat down, his father, Franco Mazzavini, asked snidely, "Have you written anything I might have read?"

The smirk on his face annoyed Beryl. She worded her response accordingly. "I've written magazine features and short stories, series for newspapers, novellas, and four biographical texts: one on Raymundo Bushkill who contributed so greatly to the development of obstetrical forceps; one on Hermione Iverson and her steadfast but unrequited love for Swami Vivekananda, Sri Ramakrishna's principal exponent; one on the tragic poet William McGonagall and his influence on modern American poetry; and one on the life of Raoul Murphy and his failed attempts to repeal the infield fly rule. I propose to examine a benign instance of common nationality acting as an irresistible force in the bonding of two disparate professionals, that is to say, Massimiliano Mazzavini and Giovanni Calvino. It's not exactly the sort of work you pick up and can't put down."

"Shall we dance?" Martin pointedly asked, speaking, unfortunately, only a moment before the orchestra began to play *People will Say We're In Love* and Massimiliano insisted that Beryl dance with him. He danced extremely well and occasionally paused to sing a line or two. Beryl knew most of the words and joined him in the refrain. Since he was the guest of honor and this was his party, everyone stopped dancing to watch them skim across the floor with steps that sometimes would glide and at others would nearly hop. He held her unusually close but fortunately she was able to keep up with him without tripping or falling or missing a beat or having her sari come loose, a not unheard of disaster.

At the end of the dance everyone, including the bandleader, applauded. As a joke, Massimiliano bowed and Beryl curtsied deeply; and the two left the dance floor.

In a voice that everyone could hear, 'Nana' Mazzavini leaned towards Beryl and said, "Look at the color in my husband's face. He hasn't looked this good in months. I hope you take a very long time to write your book and that we have dinner and dancing at the club at least once or twice a week."

"They'll run out of old songs to play," Martin said looking sternly at his grandfather. "They only played these weird numbers because you asked them to. Thank God, you're not a hundred tonight or we'd be treated to *Alice Blue Gown*."

"*Maestro!*" Massimiliano called to the bandleader, "My grandson Martin Mazzavini, the famous criminal defense attorney, has a request, *Alice Blue Gown*, in waltz time, if you would."

Martin glared at him and did not move. Massimiliano extended his hand to Beryl. "I'm the only man in my family who can handle a waltz. Perhaps before you finish your book you would be kind enough to teach my grandson."

"Sir... I will do my best... but one can only play the hand one is dealt."

"He does too much of that already," the elderly gentleman said as he began to lead Beryl in a waltz and Martin covered his face, laughing and shaking his head.

When they returned to the table, Beryl was about to say, "That is enough dancing for me," when Ronald Calvino approached her to ask her to dance. She could not decline.

The orchestra began to play, *Tie A Yellow Ribbon Round The Old Oak Tree* which ordinarily would have been a difficult number to dance to, except that Ronald Calvino was as good a dancer as the guest of honor. Everyone at the table got up to dance except Martin.

"How is the investigation coming along?" Ronald asked.

"I can't chew gum and dance," Beryl said. "Ask me when we're finished."

The music ended and Ronald took Beryl's arm and led her to his table. She met Lucille again, and Stephanie and Ronald, Jr. Lucille asked, "How is the research coming along?" And before Beryl could answer, she informed the others that Beryl was a famous author... "a famous research type author."

"What or whom are you researching?" Stephanie asked.

"Giovanni Calvino and Massimiliano Mazzavini. I'm exploring nationality as a bonding factor between two disparate professionals."

Ronald Calvino quickly entered the conversation to mitigate some of the peculiarity of the explanation. "I've heard about it. You're not doing the topic justice. It's going to be one helluva docu-fiction or whatever you call the biography. Those were two extraordinary men." He turned to Stephanie. "An author doesn't like to give too much away."

"Book Schmook," Stephanie said. "What I'd like to know is where on earth did you get that sari? It is fabulous."

"In Paramaribo, Suriname. A lady from India has a silk shop there and she also sells a few saris. I saw this and fell in love with it. A friend of mine bought it for me to wear to a special function that was being given in his honor."

"That's Dutch Guiana," Stephanie said. "I'm intrigued. What was the special event?"

"A party at the Japanese Embassy. I could tell you more but then--"

"You'd have to kill me." The two women laughed. "I want to read your book when it's finished - and if there is anything I can do by way of helping you with your research, don't hesitate to ask me. I'm in public relations. We have our methods."

It was an enjoyable encounter and as Ronald took Beryl back to the Mazzavini table, a pretty blonde girl was pulling Martin out onto the dance floor.

"That's his ex," Franco Mazzavini explained. "Good family. His mother and I hoped he'd settle down, but he says Claudia didn't want to get married so she broke off the relationship."

Beryl looked at the two of them. The girl was looking up at Martin with adoring eyes. "It's probably for the best. I think he wants to be a family man, but taking care of a family is a huge task when a man is trying to become established in his profession."

"Absolutely," Massimiliano concurred but would not go along with the fiction of blame. "He would be spending too many nights at the office or going out of town too many times. And when he was at home it would be phone calls and briefs that had to be written. If she can't understand that now, there's little hope that she'd understand it when she was a captive audience as his wife. Maybe even with a baby or two."

Beryl noticed that while Martin was an extremely graceful dancer, he had a decidedly bored expression on his face. As the end of the dance, he escorted Claudia back to her table and left her there.

Franco Mazzavini took Beryl's arm. "My son Martin would probably like to do the honors," he said, "but let's let him sit awhile. I have the feeling you'd like to meet Lorenzo Calvino and his family who are sitting right across the room. Would you like to meet them," he asked.

"But of course," she said. Franco led her to Lorenzo's table. She noticed immediately how differently the members of his party were dressed. Everything about the women was garish and exaggerated: the hair styles, heavy makeup, acrylic nails, spike heels, jewelry, and garments. Neither Lorenzo nor his two sons stood up. "This lady," said Franco, "has been commissioned to write a biography of your brother and my father. They were good friends and she's a talented writer. It ought to be a great book."

"Fiction?" said Lorenzo.

"Ah, necessity is the mother of invention. I hope I get all the facts and won't have to resort to making nasty guesses," Beryl replied, smiling.

Franco waved a hand at the group of staring faces and led Beryl back to his table just in time for Dino to approach with a camera. Massimiliano, Franco, and Martin pushed their chairs in line and smiled. Beryl stood behind Dino and pronounced, "Max, Frank, and Marty. The legal profession's answer to Tinker to Evers to Chance."

SUNDAY, JANUARY 8, 2012

Beryl, Martin, and Sensei rented a car in Oaxaca on Sunday evening and bought two six-packs of Coke and packaged pastries so that they could leave the city before dawn and drive the mountain highway to Tehuantepec. Sensei was behind the wheel. "If they straightened this road out, it would stretch to Lima, Peru," he said as he negotiated the curves.

The sun had just risen over the mountains as they passed Tlacolula de Matamoros. There had been little traffic even for a Monday morning, and as they drove along the road that had been notched out of a mountain's side, the mist in the valleys had given them a sense of peaceful separation from the world below. And then, a moment after they turned one particularly sharp curve, they found the road blocked by a long, telephone pole that lay across it. "This is trouble," Sensei said. There were boulders on both sides of the road. "The thugs are probably hiding behind those rocks." He slowed the car to a stop. Beryl made sure her tennis shoes were securely tied.

Sensei and Martin got out of the car and went to move the obstacle from the roadway. As they bent to pick up one end of the pole to pivot it around its opposite end, four armed men emerged from behind the boulders and confronted them.

"*Habla español, amigo?*" the leader asked Sensei.

"No," Sensei answered.

"*Donde va?* Where you go?"

"Tehuantepec." Sensei looked around and saw Beryl get out of the car.

"*Que pasa?*" she called, using two of the few dozen words she knew. She had seen the shadow of someone behind a boulder at the side of

74

the road. She walked to it and looked behind it to see a man with an AK47 hiding there. "*Ola!*" she called. "*Buenos dias.*" He pointed the gun at her and gestured that she should return to the road. As she did, he followed her.

Beryl and Sensei did a quick risk assessment of the opponents who faced them. All five men appeared to be semi-intoxicated or sluggish from a hangover. Their eyes were bleary and the corners of their mouths were clogged with old saliva.

"You got money?" the leader asked Sensei.

"A little money. Just Traveler's Cheques."

"Give me money." The man with the AK47 walked to Martin and poked him in his chest with the weapon's barrel.

Martin looked at Sensei for an indication of what he should do. Beryl raised her arms and called, "*Un momento.*" She and Sensei were moving to the eastern side of the highway.

Martin realized what they were trying to do. "*Por favor,*" he said to the man with the Kalashnikov, and, with his hands held high, he began to walk backwards towards Sensei and Beryl. "I played football at Cornell," he said to Sensei and Beryl. "I wasn't varsity, but I was considered a good tackle."

Sensei pretended to be gathering their money. He took out a pocket full of change. "The easiest one to tackle is the Kalashnikov," he said. "He can't point it at you if you're up close. Ok. On the count of five, Beryl, you take the two on the right and I'll take the two on the left."

"Five?" Martin asked.

Beryl pretended to be on the verge of crying. "Oh..." she wimpered, "we have an old French joke we use. 'There were three cats sitting in a rowboat. The rowboat overturned and *une, deux, trois, quatre, cinq.*' When you hear Sensei yell '*une*' in French, just continue the count and when the cats sink, you act."

The men were getting impatient with waiting, but they seemed to pay no attention to the sun that was shining in their eyes. "Hey!" one called. "You get money now!"

Martin began to walk towards the man who had poked him. "*Señor!*" he called. "*Quantos?*"

Beryl and Sensei stood side by side and then slowly began to walk toward the men. "*No tenemos dinero,*" Beryl said in a whining, helpless voice. "*Somos pobres.*" Then she turned to Sensei and asked in a suffering tone, "Is that '*somos*' or '*estamos*' - I never can remember."

"*Une!*" Sensei called. And Beryl and Martin mentally completed the count to *cinq*.

Martin lunged at the man with the AK47, and the man's trigger finger contracted as he fell backwards. The gun fired and several bullets struck two of the men who confronted Beryl and Sensei. The other two men stood in complete confusion as Beryl and Sensei kicked them with swinging leg strikes that knocked them backwards onto the road. As one stumbled and got to his feet, he tried to get his revolver from his holster. Sensei struck him fiercely in the throat, sending him sprawling onto the ground. Beryl, too, struck her opponent under his chin, snapping his head back so forcefully that she could hear his neck break. Martin had taken the assault weapon away from the man who lay on the asphalt, and in a spontaneous move, he took the weapon and hit the stock against the man's forehead.

Martin looked at Sensei and Beryl. "That was way too easy," he said. "Are we sure no one else is around?"

They looked around and saw no one else. "What do you call those kicks?" Martin asked.

Sensei smiled. "Do you want to learn how to do them? If so they're called *geri*. You'll need a few years of practice. But you did ok with that tackle skill. You got three of them. We only got one each."

"Let's do a casualty count." Beryl checked the men. "Two dead. Two wounded by the Kalash, and one with blunt force trauma to the temple. He's dead or out cold. Get their weapons."

She went to the car and emptied out an overnight bag. Martin and Sensei put the guns inside the bag and as much of the Kalashnikov as could fit inside it. The barrel stuck out ominously. "The gun was hot," Martin noted.

"It had just been fired," Sensei said. "Get it? Fired."

"Oh, now what?" Martin still had not processed the event.

"Now we load the living men into the car and we drive them to the nearest town and then we prepare to be arrested and detained for God knows how long. This, after all, is Mexico," Beryl said angrily.

"Why are you upset?" Martin asked.

"Because you weren't supposed to be here. You're my responsibility."

"I saved your life!" Martin protested.

"It is entirely possible that you will regret doing that by the time the *policia* get finished with us."

Martin tried to think of a way to avoid dealing with the police. "Leave the son of a bitches here. Take their weapons and dump them a mile down the road."

Sensei spoke quietly. "We can't leave wounded men to die in the sun."

"We all have phones," Martin countered. "We can call and ask for help. I didn't intend to abandon them completely."

A truck came around the curve. Martin waved it down. "Do you speak English?" he asked.

"A little," the driver answered.

"Can you give these men a ride to the next town? A couple of them need to get to a hospital. I'll give you fifty dollars American."

"Sure... put them in the back and move that pole."

Sensei and Beryl looked at each other and shrugged. "Let's go get 'em," Sensei said.

He and Martin carried the men to the truck bed. When they had loaded all five, they removed the pole from the road. Martin got in the truck bed with the men. Sensei returned to the car and started it, and Beryl, carrying the bag of weapons, got in the passenger's seat of the cab. The driver saw the barrel of the Kalashnikov sticking out, but since it was pointed away from him and she had both hands in view, he seemed to think nothing of it.

"Where you go?" the driver asked.

"To Tehuantepec," Beryl replied.

"It's good we go to Tehuantepec," the driver said. "I got cases of fruit back there. If we stay to explain in next town, they get bad."

"I understand," Beryl said.

They passed through small towns without stopping and arrived in Tehuantepec at a hospital. One by one they unloaded the men. A hospital attendant left the dead lying on the sidewalk while he tended to the wounded.

"*Ladrones*," Beryl said. "*Vamos a la policia ahorita.*"

The attendant seemed to understand as she held up the bag of weapons.

They walked to the police station. "Please God," Martin said, "Let somebody there speak English."

It required more than an hour for Captain Martinez to discover what had occurred. He motioned to Sensei. "You come with me." He pointed at Beryl and Martin and ordered his subordinates to keep them sitting there. "You two stay here until we get back."

Beryl noticed *Se Busca* posters on the wall. "Wanted," she said to Martin. "Just like in the Old West. So... how do you feel after your first brush with death, "*Under the Volcano.*"

"What volcano?" he asked.

"It's the title of a book about Mexico. Popocatepetl, the Sleeping Maiden.. that's the volcano outside Mexico City. It's about an alcoholic's adventures on the Day of the Dead... their Halloween. Good book. If you survive, you should read it."

"I'll wait for the movie."

"They already made a movie of it. Your grandmother's right. You need to get out of the house more."

Sensei and Captain Martinez went to the hospital. One of the men who had been shot had died. "This man..." the Captain said as he pulled the sheet down from the dead man's face, "Who killed him?"

"The young man who was with us. He tackled the man with the AK47. The man was holding the gun with his finger on the trigger and when he went down the gun fired several rounds, hitting two of the men. This man was one of them."

"This man has a big price on his head. He killed the daughter of a rancher here. Her father will give him 12,000 pesos for killing him. That's about a thousand dollars, American."

"I doubt that he'll accept it, but I'll tell him."

"The others have no price on their heads.... but they are all bad *hombres*. You did us a favor. *Gracias*."

It was the last thing that Sensei expected to hear. They returned to the station.

The captain kept his arm around Sensei's shoulder when they entered. He spoke to his men in a low voice. One of the officers picked up a telephone and called someone. The party answered and the Captain spoke to him. Martin and Beryl kept silent. The Captain put Sensei on the phone. Sensei had no idea what the person he was listening to was saying. As Sensei shrugged his shoulders indicating his befuddlement, the captain whispered, "He's thanking you. Just say 'It was my pleasure'... something like that."

Sensei looked at Beryl and Martin. "How do you say, 'It was my pleasure?'"

"*Avec plaisir*," Martin answered.

As Sensei repeated "*Avec plaisir*," Beryl poked Martin. "That's French, you fool!"

Unfortunately, the man to whom Sensei spoke, also spoke French and he launched a long torrent of expressions of gratitude in French. Sensei covered the mouthpiece, "He's speaking French to me!"

Beryl said, "When he's finished, just say, "*Merci beaucoup*." When the man finished, Sensei repeated, *Merci beaucoup*, and put the Captain back on the phone.

The captain tried to conceal his merriment. This was a story he could tell for years. When he hung up the telephone he said, "No offense... but the man who asked me to give you the reward money is grateful to God that a Frenchman - not an American - got the killer."

In Spanish, the Captain related the story to his men, and while they all laughed good naturedly at the story, the Captain opened a safe that stood in the corner of the room and removed an envelope that contained a check for 12,000 pesos. He took a form from his desk drawer and handed it to Martin. "You fill this out... you earned this money. It's a reward for killing that man."

Martin accepted the document and took a pen from his shirt pocket. "I'll make a deal with you," he said. "You can have this money to do with it anything you want... if you'll help us to find a document about a man's suicide that happened here forty years ago. Do you still have those files?"

"Yes... but they are down in the basement. The men don't like to go down there... too many rats."

Martin took out his wallet and removed two one hundred dollar bills which he concealed from view, allowing only the Captain to see them. "Will this help to overcome their fears. Or your inconvenience?"

"Yes... I'll get a flashlight."

Beryl nudged Sensei. "Say what you will... the kid is sharp."

As soon as the Captain turned the light on, roaches of a dozen varieties, scattered across the floor into the shadows. The rats were more brazen and ran along the pipes and the tops of the old filing cabinets. The room bore the stench of dead insects and rodents, urine and feces. "You could use a puma down here," Martin said.

The Captain laughed. "Don't think we didn't try that once. He got sick and died."

"Poisoned rats?"

"Exactly. The poisoned rats had also eaten poisoned roaches."

"Poor cat."

The drawer marked 1971 yielded the file marked "Paolo Calvino." The captain carried it upstairs as Martin followed, sending rats on the steps scampering.

It contained a photograph. "Jesus," said Martin. "He looks like Dean. That is one strong family resemblance." He turned to the Captain. "May I copy this photo?"

"I'll have it scanned and sent." He summoned his clerk. Martin gave him his business card. "He can use this address.... and if it's not too much trouble, to this one, too." He laid Beryl's card on the desk. In a few moments the scan of Paolo's image appeared on Beryl's laptop and Martin's phone.

"The record says that he committed suicide on December 10th, 1971. Death by drowning. Did you know that he had been... I don't know the word in English."

Beryl made a scissors movement with her index and middle finger. "Yes. A tragic accident."

"Indeed." He sighed. "Is there anything specific you want to know??"

"We're looking for a piece of paper on which he had written a kind of suicide note... it was a poem."

The captain looked through the typed forms. "I'm sorry," he said. "There's nothing else here."

Martin took the file and surreptitiously placed the two one hundred dollar bills in it and handed it to the Captain. "Here, with our thanks."

Beryl asked, "Is there anyone around who might remember the incident?"

The Captain thought for a long moment. "A couple of widows of men who were here at that time. But not anyone who would have encountered the document." He took the money and then hesitated. "Martin," he said, joking, "I'll give you two hundred dollars if you go down and put the file back."

Everyone laughed. Martin signed for the receipt of the reward, endorsed the back of the check, returned it to the Captain, and shook hands. "Can you tell us where his grave is?"

"Yes... We can go in my vehicle."

Beryl stopped at a roadside vendor who sold flowers. She bought a bouquet to put on the grave. At the cemetery gate, the Captain asked the caretaker where the grave of Paolo Calvino was, and he led them directly to it. The grave, along with all the others, had recently been mowed by the caretaker. Beryl laid the flowers in front of the headstone that was simply marked, "Paolo Calvino, 1939-1971" and took photos to give to Lucille.

They said a brief prayer and returned to the police station, said goodbye to the Captain, and got into their car.

"Well," Beryl said when they were safely back on the highway, "That was exciting."

"Let's eat," Sensei said, "and get the hell out of here."

Before nightfall they were back in Oaxaca.

Lying on her bed, Beryl thought aloud. "We could have done a few things that would have gotten us nowhere. We could have asked the newspaper office if they had anything in their morgue files. Someone might have given the poem to a newspaperman because it was in English and the Captain wasn't around then. The person most likely to speak English would have been a newspaperman. Or, we could have gone to the military - since they might have thought that this was some kind of recorded accusation of American prisoner abuse. In neither case would we have gotten the document. And in one of the two cases, we'd likely have been detained. We go next to Mexico City." She turned to Sensei. "will you be going directly home?"

"Yes," he said. "I have to get back."

"We'll go to Houston. We need to search the records in Texas City."

TUESDAY, JANUARY 10, 2012

It was sunny and warm and except for the acrid smell of oil that clogged the air and the burn-off that left a film on their windshield, the drive to the recorder's office in Galveston County was pleasant.

Beryl approached the desk clerk and told her that she and Martin were trying to find a parcel of land purchased in 1971. "It would have been a large parcel of land, suitable for an airport."

"We have a famous parcel that was sold at that time. It's still the object of cocktail party chatter. I'm gonna' take a shot and see if I hit it." She pulled an old canvas covered plat book from the archives' shelf and carried it to the counter top. She turned a half-dozen pages and said, "Here it is. 1280 acres of land at $1,000. per acre. One Million Two Hundred Eighty Thousand dollars. The land wasn't worth a hundred dollars an acre. It's mostly swamp, depending on the time of year. No rights of way were obtained. The man who sold it retired on Ambergris Key with servants and a fine house. He loves the Caribbean. Last we heard his family was doing fine."

"Who bought the land?" Martin asked.

"A company incorporated in the Commonwealth of Kentucky." She put her reading glasses on. "Calgec Development."

"What happened to the land?"

"It was auctioned off by the county. Taxes had not been paid. Then somebody paid fifty thousand dollars for part of the tract. Then we had a major hurricane... and it was underwater for a spell and finally the county took it over. There was a reclamation program pushed through the legislature and the land was reclaimed. It was sold off in 1995 to a developer. There's houses on it now."

"Well, thank you very much. Is there any chance we could get copies of the supportive documents?" Martin asked.

"Well, honey, I'd like to help you but those files are buried... down in the basement. Don't ask me why people store things in basements. They ought to put the old files in the attic. They're safer there."

"Unless the roof leaks," Martin said, smiling.

"And ain't that just life, honey? If it doesn't get you on the bottom, it gets you on the top."

There was no charge for the information. Beryl and Martin returned to the airport to wait for the next flight to Chicago.

On the plane back to Chicago, Beryl and Martin compared notebooks. "When I had brunch with Lucille, she mentioned that Paolo only wanted to be a bean farmer.... that's what she said. He wanted to get enough money together to get a house and farm equipment like a tractor, and he needed to buy land in the Southwest. I'm thinking about Jojoba... In the financial events of the time, a lot of people got rich selling farmland to raise jojoba beans. The oil from the beans was supposed to be a substitute for whale oil. The "back to nature" type of wildlife preservation enthusiasts - which sound like Paolo's bedfellows - got very excited about jojoba beans."

"I never heard of them," Martin said.

"There have been a few passing references to Paolo's being a dreamer. Those jojoba bean farmers mostly went belly-up. We'll have to ask Lucille if it was jojoba farming he was interested in. This is just a point of interest. It doesn't really matter except that it shows the zeitgeist. That entrepreneurial imagination that temporarily vivified dead minds."

"So," Martin said, "now that we know Lorenzo's corporation bought land foolishly and borrowed the money from the congenial Mr. Greco, what have we actually learned?"

"Nothing.. We just verified what we were told by an inmate. This means only that Greco's men were not likely to be Paolo's torturers. But Lorenzo was the one who delivered him to those torturers, presumably the Nievo family. Lucille said that she could tell he grew more and more frantic as the days passed. Perhaps he feared that Paolo had been killed."

"Or he expected him to break under the pressure and to reveal... what? Parini said that Paolo never saw those maps. We don't know what was on them."

"Lorenzo obviously planted them." Martin sighed. "Son of a bitch."

"I'm inclined to agree that he planted the maps. But it is unlikely that he would have put the Texas City type of sites on the map. We don't even know if they were Geologic Survey Maps. All he said was 'maps.'"

"The Nievo family is all broken up, I think. That's something else we have to look into."

"Let's suppose," Beryl said, "that Lorenzo fed Paolo bogus landing sites and he assumed that Paolo would break under pressure and reveal them; and then his competition would buy land at those bogus sites and get burned bad, leaving him to scout out the best sites around what he figured were the real sites. It would be nice to know who told him the names of those "real" sites and it would also be nice to know Lorenzo's connection to the Nievo family. Was he a conspirator or a competitor. He had to have a connection since he delivered Paolo to them. I don't for one minute believe that baloney about dropping him off at an inn upstate. But I think we're getting too far afield."

"Well, it all did influence Antonio's decision to disinherit Paolo. I think it's important to find out more about Calgrec's dealings."

"Naturally," Beryl said ironically, "and while we're at it, we could try to find out who is trying to kill your grandfather."

"A footnote's interest," Martin said. "What a fucking mystery this all is."

Beryl bent over and whispered in Ronald Calvino's ear, "Sorry we couldn't make it here to dust the recorder." She put on latex gloves. "I'm going to do it now."

She dusted the recorder and tape and the interior of the towel dispener's lid. With clear "lifting" tape she took off the prints. Then she took a cloth and began to wipe away all the carbon residue. She emailed the prints to George and had him run them through IAFIS.

"Let's go out for coffee, shall we?" Calvino asked. Then in a whisper he added, "My mom will be down at the coffee shop in ten minutes. She remembered a little more about the poem."

"Yes. And I'll get one of those sugar free muffins. I love those muffins," Beryl said clearly for the benefit of any recording devices. She was also glad to get out of his office.

As they waited for the elevator she told him that she had photographs of his father's body and his grave. "If you want to see them, you'll have to ask. I won't suggest that you see them. You'll have to decide that for yourself."

"I want to see them."

In the elevator she opened her laptop and showed him his father's photograph.

"He looks so peaceful lying there. So young. He reminds me of my cousin, Dino."

"Yes, that's definitely a Calvino face," Beryl agreed.

"He has that Calvino hair. Thick and sandy colored. Northern."

Lucille Calvino, wearing a new winter coat and scarf around her head, sat in the coffee shop, drinking a latte. "I'm getting spoiled with all this fancy coffee," she said as they approached her table.

"It can get fattening if you eat the muffins with it." Beryl sat down as Ronald Calvino and Martin went to get their order. "I'll have what you have," she told Martin, "plus the muffin." She laid her hand on Lucille's hand.. "We were in Tehuantepec day before yesterday. We saw your husband's file and the Captain of the police department scanned his morgue photograph. I've showed Ronald, but I want to ask you in advance if you want to see it. Think it over."

"I'd like to see it very much."

Beryl opened her laptop and showed her the large picture of Paolo's body.

"Ah," Lucille gasped. "He looks so peaceful and contented. Like he's sleeping. So young and strong. What a beautiful man he was."

"I'll send this through to Ronald. You two can decide what you want to do with the image. Now... what is that line about the poem you remembered?"

Ronald and Martin came with the coffees and all conversation stopped until the sugar and cream were added and everyone was seated with a pastry and coffee. "I told you that in the poem he talks about himself as if he were someone else. I remembered," Lucille began, "that I had been puzzled about the opening line. I had remembered it as, 'This song is about Paolo.' But I woke up this morning and the line popped into my mind. The opening line was, 'I sing of Paolo.' Does that make sense?"

Beryl closed her eyes and said, "Oh, Lord." She opened her laptop and searched for e.e. cummings' poem, *I Sing of Olaf*.

Beryl showed the screen to Lucille. "Substitute Paolo for Olaf. Is this what you read?"

Lucille burst into tears. "Yes... yes... I remember that line.... "straightway the silver bird looked grave" I didn't know what it meant?"

Ronald turned the screen and read the poem. "After all these years of wondering."

"Nice work," Martin said. "You've earned your fee."

"Well, Paolo Calvino had good taste in poetry. e.e. cummings was a fine poet and this poem is particularly good."

"What is the 'silver bird'?" Lucille asked.

"The insignia that a colonel wears. There are bars, and oak leaf clusters, eagles, and stars... they all indicate rank," Beryl explained. "I'm no authority... it's something like that."

Ronald read the last lines of the poem. "*Christ, of his mercy infinite, I pray to see; and Olaf, too, preponderatingly because unless statistics lie, he was more brave then me, more blond than you.*"

Everyone sat in silence, not eating or drinking until Beryl broke the 'stop-action' moment. "Here are photographs of his grave," she said, turning towards Lucille the screen that showed the photographs. "I'll see to it that you get copies of these photographs, too.

"Well, now we know. I couldn't imagine why your dad thought it was the Army that was persecuting him. Clearly, it was one of the Mafia families who wanted that information about the landing sites."

"Do you know which one?" Ronald asked.

"They're all dead by now," Martin said. "What we need to focus on is what all this has to do with my grandfather. And also, the same people who tormented your father are now possibly after you. There's an undercurrent of evil. We have to find out why your father was tormented and make it public."

A look of alarm passed over Lucille Calvino's face. Beryl noted it and said, "It's enough to know what it is and see to it that the proof is in safe hands. That's just intellectual satisfaction. What we need to know is who is bugging Ronald's office and who is trying to kill Mr. Massavini."

"At least," Lucille allowed, "we now know the poem. I will have Ron print it out for me... maybe he will substitute Paolo's name for Olaf's, and he can send you a copy."

"I'd like that," Beryl said. "Incidentally, you mentioned bean farming... was that jojoba beans?"

"Yes... Paolo was convinced that he could make a living finding a substitute for whale oil."

"Your husband must have been a wonderful man."

"He was. I think of him every day."

Beryl finished her coffee and muffin. "And now we have to get going." A call came in on her cellphone. She got up and walked away from the table to answer it. George was calling to tell her that the prints on the recorder were not in the system.

She returned to the table. "I need you," she said to Ronald, "to leave a book with a new jacket that's been completely wiped down on your desk just before you leave your office and the cleaning lady comes in. Leave it in such a way that she'll pick it up and handle it. Also get another book with a perfectly wiped down jacket and hand it to your secretary and ask her to tell you how many editions there are. Tell her you forgot your reading glasses. Tell her anything. I need her prints, too. And we can look at things on Dino's desk to see if the unknown prints are his."

"I'll get those prints for you, today. Will it matter if mine are on them, too."

"Sure... that's why I'm going to take your prints right now." She removed print sheets from her tote bag and made him leave a full set of prints as his exemplar.

Martin's secretary had located the Ruggieri family. Beryl took the number and went into Martin's office and called it from his land line. He lay on the couch while she spoke to an elderly lady who identified herself as the widow of Alonzo Ruggieri.

"I'm wondering, Mrs. Ruggieri, if I brought you some of those superb Italian pastries from the bakery in the mall here, if you'd let me have a few minutes of your time to interview you. I'm writing a book about Giovanni Calvino and Massimiliano Mazzavini."

"You gonna bring Massimiliano with you?"

"No, but I can bring his handsome grandson. Will he do?"

"Yes but he has to make up the difference with *Cannoli, Taralli. Bocconotti, Rum Savoia,* Parigini. He's a good Italian boy. He'll know. I'm gonna make tea. How soon you get here?"

Beryl asked Martin how long it would take to pick up the pastries and get to the Ruggieri house. "Forty-five minutes," he called.

She heard his response. "I'm gonna look for you and that pastry in forty-five minutes." She hung up the telephone.

Mrs. Alonzo Ruggieri stood waiting behind the front door window of her dilapidated house. As soon as Martin parked, she opened the door. Beryl had also brought a box of Italian chocolates. Martin carried in four boxes of pastries. He had spent sixty dollars at the bakery.

The old lady began to eat the cannoli ravenously. She was thin and appeared not to have eaten in a few days. "Do you have a grocery store nearby?" Beryl asked.

"Yes... but he don't sell to me no more." She poured weak tea into three cups.

"Why not?"

"I owe him too much money."

"You look like a smart lady," Martin said. "If you help us, we'll help you. I'll go pay that grocery bill after we conclude our interview. Deal?"

"Sure. I tell you anyway. But if you wanna take care of my bill, I'm not gonna complain."

When she had finished her fourth pastry, she sipped her tea. "My husband, Alonzo, he died in Stateville. When he went to jail twenty years ago, he didn't rat on nobody, and the family is supposed to take care of me. For a few years, yeah... I got a little money every month. But then they stop. How I'm gonna live? We have three kids and they give me what they can. Each one says, 'Ma, sell this house and move in with me.' But I know how that goes. I have friends. They sell their house and move in with a son or daughter and their life is hell. Alonzo agrees with me. He hears stories, too, about a mother who must move into her kid's house. It ain't good.

"Alonzo has a better idea. He tells me to stay in this house because he's gonna mail me his memoirs. I will get money by selling the book. He's afraid that the guards will take his copybooks when they search the cell. Contraband, they call it. And then they sell the book or give it to the D.A. Every week I get a letter from him. On the front of the page, is a letter. On the back is his memoirs. He even numbered the back pages so I don't mix them up. He don't want his letters to go no place else. So I don't sell the house.

"His first letters are about his life as a boy on the streets, but you wanna know about those Calvinos. My Alonzo can tell ya' plenty. He writes everything what Lorenzo Calvino and Lucca Farinella and the Nievo family did to Paolo Calvino. Then he died and I don't get any more letters." She opened another box and cut a piece of the rum savoia. Beryl and Martin patiently waited while she slowly savored the flavor with her eyes closed.

"Do you have the letters about Paolo?" Beryl asked.

"No. What I'm gonna do with half a book? I call up Giovanni and tell him I got letters from Alonzo that make Giovanni and Antonio look real bad for what they did to Paolo. He laughs. Then I read him about that Easter Sunday dinner and what the Nievos did to Paolo. He don't laugh no more. He came right here. Sat where you're sittin'. I said, 'You want these letters? You come back with money.' He said, 'How much?' I said ten thousand. That's what I sold them for. He looks like a rat in those letters. I could'a got more. But what I'm gonna do? My taxes were due on the house. I owed a lot of money. He gave me the money. I paid my bills. He said he gonna give me more, but then he died. I didn't make no copies. Just as well. If Lorenzo knew I had copies, he'd kill me for them."

"What did it say about Lorenzo?" Martin asked.

Maria Ruggiero swallowed the last bite of the slice of cake she was holding and then laughed with a guttural acknowledgement. "Huh! *Marone*! What a snake that Lorenzo is. He had a friend, Lucca, who is nephew of old man Nievo. Lucca has some kinda grudge against Nievo. Lucca and Lorenzo are more than good friends... how much more I don't know. Alonzo thought they maybe was very 'special' friends and Nievo don't like no 'special' friends. Anyway, Lucca tells Lorenzo that he has inside information about where the government is gonna build new airplane terminals for those Concorde planes. They can make big money if they buy the land before any competition finds out. So Lorenzo's wife... she's Salvatore Greco's daughter... she goes and starts to buy the land. Then they find out the Nievo family is already interested in getting the land. The Nievos wanna know what these secret locations are. This puts Lucca on the spot. He says he don't know nothin', 'but the Calvinos, they know.' Lorenzo knows Paolo is looking for land he wanna buy for farming; so he acts like he could use Paolo's advice. He tells him about the airport terminals - the places they gonna build those SST airports. Only he gives fake locations to Paolo. And he makes a plan to use Paolo to give bad information to the Nievos. He thinks that Paolo is weak, and if he gets a little pinch he will say, 'Ouch, I'm gonna tell you want you wanna know.'

"But that Lorenzo! Hah! A snake! He tells Paolo to guard those town names with his life. Lorenzo promises that when he makes money he will give Paolo a big payoff for him and his wife and kids. Paolo has a new baby, a couple years old... and he likes this idea. He wanna buy a farm in Arizona. That's all he wants. Lorenzo gonna get him that farm. If anybody asks him, he must tell them there ain't any new sites... just additions to terminals they have now. What a snake! He thinks Paolo is gonna break down and tell them the phony names.

"And Monica Greco Calvino just happens to let it slip out that Paolo knows the names of the towns they gonna build those airplane terminals. All this time Lorenzo is borrowing money from his father-in-law, Greco, and is buying up the land around the places that Lucca had told him were the real locations.

"Lorenzo and Lucca arrange for Paolo to be picked up by Nievo on Easter Sunday. Alonzo says he puts a Mickey Finn in his drink and Paolo wakes up trussed up like a turkey. He's gotta hood on his head and he don't know who's got him. Day after day they torment him and do bad things to him... put electricity down there... you know where. But Paolo doesn't give away the locations that *lucertola* Lorenzo told him were the real ones." She made a zig-zagging lizard like movement with her hand on its way to the box of chocolates. She opened the box and removed a chocolate which she paused in her narrative to eat. While she chewed a caramel, she pushed the open box to Beryl. "These ain't no five and dime chocolates. Try one." Beryl and Martin both took a caramel and the three of them sat at the table and chewed for a few minutes before Maria was ready to resume telling the details of the story her husband had told her in his memoirs.

"Antonio Calvino wants to know where Paolo is. He don't show up for work. Where is he? His wife don't know. Lorenzo lies and says that Paolo is buyin' land in Arizona. Antonio asks him where Paolo get that kinda money. Lorenzo says that he's got some kind of business going with Nievo. Antonio don't like to hear this. Antonio don't like no Mafia comin' near the Calvino family. He got enough just keepin' Greco away. He can't believe that Paolo would do that to him... go behind his back and work for Nievo.

"So, here comes Lorenzo the snake. When Paolo is finally home, Lorenzo arranges for Lucca, Nievo's nephew, to meet Paolo on the street where Antonio can see them. He set him up good. Everybody knew Paolo was lookin' to buy land so he's easy to blame for everything. Antonio is an honest man and don't want nothin' to do with that Black Hand Mafia business. He right away fires Paolo.

"Lucca and Lorenzo tell everybody that Paolo is the one who had the contact on the inside. When you're in that stock sellin' business, you don't want no 'inside' information talk goin' around. Then the government announces there will be no new airports anywhere for those planes, and Nievo and Greco have both invested in very bad deals which they say Paolo Calvino touted them onto. Antonio wanna kill Paolo with his own hands. Italian temper. We all got 'em.

"Lucca tells Giovanni and Antonio - he swears on his mother's grave - that he begged Lorenzo not to listen to Paolo, but Lorenzo said, 'He's my brother. He would never lie to me.' So in the end Paolo gets blamed for being selfish and stupid and weak."

"What happened to Lucca?" Beryl asked.

"Some fisherman found him floating face-down in Lake Erie. Maybe the Nievos learned what a big rat he was."

"When was it that you sold these pages to Giovanni Calvino?" Martin asked.

"Last August. He gave me ten thousand dollars. Then he died. That's some family, that Calvino family. They all are rats." She corrected herself. "Except Paolo. And he couldn't be buried in a Catholic cemetery, but the others could. He's the only one a saint would wanna lie next to. The others belong in hell." She poured more tea and attacked another *cannoli*.

Martin got up. "You finish up here," he said to Beryl. "I'll go down to the grocery store and pay the bill."

"You got good blood in you," Mrs. Ruggieri declared. "Your grandfather is a great man. You remember that." She turned to Beryl and whispered, "You shoulda seen that man thirty years ago. *Marone!* He was so handsome! And he could dance!"

"I know," Beryl said. "I know."

Beryl buckled her seat belt. "It is time," she said emphatically, "that we confront your grandfather. This has gone as far as we can take it without his cooperation."

"Be gentle with him."

"How gentle do you want me to be when you've asked me to rescue a drowning man? Do you want me to say, 'Please let me help you get to dry land'?"

WEDNESDAY, JANUARY 11, 2012

Beryl and Martin both slept until ten o'clock. Martin got up first and awakened her when he made coffee.

"What time is it?" she called.

"Time to eat scrambled eggs and toast and coffee and whatever else I can find in the freezer."

"I'm going to call your grandfather at home and tell him we'll be there after lunch."

"You still don't know who bugged Ronald's office. Shouldn't we find that out first?"

"Sure we should, if Ronald has the prints ready. But remember, it doesn't have to be the same person. For all we know the person who is bugging the office is just doing industrial spying. Calvino Investment is a commercial entity. This is a pivotal time in management. I'm not ruling out a connection; but I'm not hanging all my expectations on it, either. Don't worry. I'm calling Ronald Calvino now to see if he got the prints."

Beryl called Ronald's private line. "Hi, Mr. Calvino," she said. "I really want to get finished with that story about those summer vacations. Did you happen to get a look at those two books I left?"

"Yes, and they were interesting. Do you need to have them back today? If so, we can meet for lunch."

"All right. We'll pick you up outside your building at exactly noon. How's that?"

Dressed in their western garb, Beryl and Martin drove his Cadillac sedan to the doorway of Ronald's building. Ronald emerged immediately, ran to the car, and jumped into the backseat. "Good thing I took off thirty pounds last year," he said. He handed Beryl a plastic shopping bag that contained two books, each in its own plastic bag.

"Good," she said. "I can do the comparison when we stop for coffee."

They drove to the highway and stopped at a fast food joint. Sitting in a booth, Beryl got out her fingerprint kit and dusted the first book. She had a good clear thumbprint from the inside of the dispenser lid and also from the book. She photographed the print and examined them side by side in her laptop. They did not match. The cleaning lady had not touched the inside of the dispenser.

She dusted the second book and got an excellent thumbprint which, when she compared them, also did not match the print in the dispenser. "The person who's bugging you," she said to Calvino, "is not your secretary or your cleaning lady. That leaves a million females... although, the size of the print looks like it belongs to a large woman or a small man. That's George's opinion, too."

They dropped Ronald off and drove the rest of the way to the Mazzavini estate in silence. The day was overcast and matched their mood. It had been a strain to know what had happened to Ronald's father and not be able to tell him.

As they turned onto the driveway, the sun suddenly broke through the clouds. The snow on the lawn glistened and the tiny branches of the hedges that lined the drive way shimmered in their transparent icicle covers. The main house's well-insulated roof prevented the snow from melting, and it looked like the subject of a Christmas card as smoke rose from the chimneys. "It's such a pretty place," Beryl said, but Martin did not answer.

Inside the house, Beryl hesitated to take her coat off. "I need to speak to you," she said quietly to Massimiliano Mazzavini. "Do you have a place we can speak in private?"

"Let me get my coat," he said. "We can walk down the driveway and see if any mail has come. Or we can sit in the gazebo."

The wind had died down and the sky had begun to show more of its blue. As they walked down the driveway, Massimiliano let his hand brush the hedges and the icicles cracked and fell to the ground. He picked up a stick and used it instead of his hand. "We used to do this as kids," he said. "We'd run a stick along picket fences. In town we'd use a piece of rebar if the fence was an iron, hairpin fence. It made a great noise. There used to be a lot of those fences.

"I used to think that Antonio Calvino was an Italian nobleman. His family was from Firenza... Florence. He lived in a big house here. I went to school with Giovanni. I thought about that family as though they were the Medici. Patrons of the arts. Explorers and traders. Saints and Popes. One of the families that made Italy great. It took me a lifetime to find out that they were ordinary people when it came to morality. There is an old Italian joke. A poor man goes to heaven, and as he stands and waits for Saint Peter to let him in, a rich man comes up to heaven and Saint Peter drops everything to welcome the rich man. Everybody makes a fuss over him. Finally, Saint Peter gets around to the poor man who says to him, 'I see that even in heaven, you get better treatment when you're rich.' Saint Peter says, 'No, my son. That's not it at all. We get poor people up here by the thousands... but do you know how rare it is to have a rich man come to the gate?' That's what money does to morality. It cheapens it."

They had reached the mailbox and there was nothing inside it. "It's still too early," Mazzavini said. "Let's go sit in the gazebo. The path's been cleared."

Martin watched from the house as they walked across to the gazebo and sat inside on the bench that ran along the railing.

"Do you know the riddle of Samson?" Mazzavini asked.

"Yes. 'Out of the eater, something to eat. Out of the strong, something that's sweet.' Ok. You've done your toastmaster thing. I think you know why I'm here."

"You're not going to let me digress my way out of confessing my guilt, are you?"

"No, I'm not. You'll tell me what I need to know. Although, I am curious about your feelings of guilt. I'm sure there's plenty of guilt to go around, but I can't imagine that very much of it would extend to you."

"Oh, I am not without my share of the guilt. I prepared Antonio's will. I never asked why his other lawyers wouldn't suffice for such a purpose. I never asked why he was disinheriting Paolo. I was young and greedy. I wanted the account. He didn't get any advice from me, and my job was to counsel. I didn't counsel. If I had talked to Antonio... the man who was an Italian Prince in my mind. If I had said, 'Let us talk about this grievance of yours against Paolo.' If I had offered to look into it and discovered for myself what the truth was and then *advised my client* the way I was supposed to, Paolo would not have killed himself. Do you know how Paolo died? Do you know why Paolo died?"

"Yes." She opened her tote bag and pulled out her laptop. "Here," she said. "Here is a photograph of his body."

Massimiliano Mazzavini stared incredulously at the photograph. "Oh, my God! Where did you get this?" He drew a breath in and shuddered, his chin quivering.

"Martin and I and Sensei Percy Wong... you remember him from Arizona, I'm sure. The three of us went to a town south of Tehuantepec where Paolo lived and was buried. The captain at the police station got it out for Martin."

"But it's forty years old! And they still had it?"

"Martin is very persuasive. It's in his blood. Besides, he killed a couple of wanted men and let the captain keep the reward money."

"*What?*"

"'What' is *what* I'm trying sideways to tell you. Martin and I know about Paolo's ordeal. We know about his castration. We know what Lorenzo did to him. And we know that the longer you keep dodging the issue, the greater the danger is to Ronald and Martin and you, of course."

"I'm not dodging the issue. Yes, I've been clinging to a straw... a faint hope that there was some mistake. Maybe Ruggieri exaggerated because Paolo had clearly blamed a military group. He wrote a poem in which he blamed the Army for his troubles. His son Ronald wrote to a friend up here right after Paolo died. He said that maybe the CIA killed him or some other paramilitary group. Without that poem - which was, essentially, a 'dying type of declaration' - how could we know whether Ruggieri was lying or exaggerating?"

"What did Giovanni specifically say?" Beryl asked.

"Giovanni had gotten Alonzo Ruggieri's letters which, he said, made everything finally make sense. He had always known that there were parts that just didn't add up. The letters were like a lens that put everything in focus and he could see clearly for the first time. He wept. I never saw a man so heartbroken by his own shame. He held the letters to his face to wipe his tears and his nose and to hide his face. My God, he was grief stricken by what he had done to his brave little brother. And to think how he had been duped by that venomous Lorenzo! I reminded him of the poem that implicated 'the Army' just to give him some hope that it wasn't really true. But he knew better."

"We know about the poem. The 'army' was, in a sense, just a metaphor. The regimented forces arrayed against him were his own family and friends. He never blamed any military group. So you've known about the poem for a long time."

"Forty years is a long time. But I remember how Giovanni and I laughed about it. We've always known... right after his son wrote to his high school buddy up here. We thought it was a further illustration of Paolo's mental state... irrational. Too much marijuana. He was a momma's boy, we thought. I think that Paolo didn't want his father to know what all had been done to him. His mother apparently knew and wanted to give him money, but Antonio wouldn't allow it so she pawned her jewelry. He also had some insurance, not much. Maybe Ronald wanted to believe that the CIA had killed his father because he couldn't bear to think he had committed suicide. We were ready to believe anything negative about Paolo."

"Well, Ronald knows what the poem is now."

"Giovanni never knew. And I don't know, either. Tell me. What is the big secret in the poem?"

Beryl opened an email that Ronald had sent in which he had substituted the name "Paolo" for the name "Olaf." "Paolo," she said, "was an anti-Vietnam war activist, so he was a conscientious objector. But the people who really hurt him weren't the thugs who tortured him. He withstood that torture trying to protect the family's secrets that had been entrusted to him. It was when he learned that his family thought so little of him that they fed him false information in the certainty that under pressure he'd spill his guts and misdirect their competitors... *that* disgrace, no man could bear. Here, read it."

Mazzavini looked at the screen. Ronald Calvino had prefaced the poem, "The Last Will and Testament of Paolo Calvino." He trembled as he read, and he quickly began to gulp and shudder, and his eyes brimmed with tears. When he reached the closing lines, his chin quivered uncontrollably and he finally began to sob. He shook so hard it was impossible to hold him or to comfort him in any way. Beryl sat beside him motionless as he gasped for breath between his violent sobs. She looked back at the house and could see Martin standing at the window.

For five minutes the old man cried, wiping his eyes and blowing his nose, unable to speak because he choked back every word with another shudder or sob. Finally, she said, "Mr. Mazzavini, we can't go back and change the past. And we can't assume that if we did or did not act in any specific way, the situation we find ourselves in today would be better or worse than it is. Some of our actions will have benefited some people and those same actions will have harmed others. The most we can ever hope for is that when we did or did not act, we weren't motivated by greed or hate or lust or any of the other seven deadly sins. That is a lofty goal and we don't always reach it. In this world, we sin and we are sinned against.

"My concern now is with Martin who is up at the house watching all this. If I know him, he's scared to death that you'll collapse under the burden of it all."

Mazzavini sat up straight. "I've never regretted anything the way I've regretted this. Forty years of calling a man a coward and a weakling. For days they tortured him, denied him water for several days at a time, didn't give him food, and still... he would not betray the brother who had ordered the torture." He began to sob again.

"Yes," Beryl said, "but sometimes things have a way of working out as if some unseen hand has shaped a destiny. Giovanni, who was so indifferent to his good brother's family, died without one of his own. Lorenzo has perhaps given rise to a 'generation of vipers' who will probably end up by biting him. And for all the abuse Paolo suffered, he alone of the three brothers had a family of whom he could be proud. And so have you. If you feel so bad about what your contribution was to the whole sordid affair, atone for it by helping Martin to become the kind of attorney you are. He loves and needs you. So get up and help that boy to develop the skill that matches his natural talent and integrity. Maybe you can find a way to bring Paolo's body back here for burial. It's sad to think that he wasn't good enough to be buried in a Catholic cemetery. But Giovanni was, and Lorenzo will be. Makes a person want to be cremated, eh?"

"If that's the only burning I experience, I'll consider myself ahead of the game." He shuddered and sighed. "Where do we go from here?" he asked.

"Ronald Calvino's office has been bugged. His telephone calls have been recorded. God knows what other spying he's been subjected to. Four attempts have been made on your life. And in trying to get to the bottom of this mystery Martin was nearly shot and killed in Mexico. So, please... let's fix this problem before anyone else is hurt."

Mazzavini stood up. "I didn't know Ronald's office was bugged."

"What's your best guess?"

"I have none! I don't know!"

"All right. It's time that we ceased worrying about things we can't change. Other things need our attention... like... who is trying to kill you? As soon as you're composed, go over the details with your attorney - that very fine attorney who's standing at the window up there. He will give you good and honest counsel."

Massimiliano Massavini followed her down the steps of the gazebo. "What is it that Martin keeps saying about you and how we're supposed to respond? *Ja, meine Konigin.*"

They sat in Massimiliano's study. Beryl and Martin each had a little blue tablet ready to make notes.

"What do you suggest is a good way for us to get Lorenzo to show his hand?" Martin said.

"First," Beryl asked, "what happened to Ruggieri's letters - the ones Giovanni bought?"

Massimiliano Mazzavini nodded and replied, "Giovanni brought them to my office when he ordered the new will. After half an hour the letters were sopping wet and full of snot and spit. He took them into the men's room and flushed them down the toilet. They're gone."

"Well," said Beryl, "they were written on copybook paper. The kind that they sell in the prison store. Nothing metal on them. We'll get a copybook and forge the letters. Are you certain that Giovanni never confronted Lorenzo?"

"Positive. He never said a word. That's why I had to invite Lorenzo to my birthday party. I didn't want him to think I knew anything that could hurt him."

"I think we should buy a few letters from Mrs. Ruggieri and then put her on a plane to Italy. Buy her some nice clothing and make sure her taxes are paid. And let her get out of town for a holiday. I'll take her to buy the clothing. You can furnish the money and airline tickets and hotel reservations.

"I think," Beryl said, "that maybe it's time for the good Mr. Mazzavini to appear at his Italian American Club, or his Knights of Columbus, or whatever Italian club he belongs to... and in a very upbeat voice that he announce that he's heard that somebody is telling damnable lies about that Paolo episode of forty years ago. Somebody has had the audacity to try to implicate Lorenzo. Mazzavini wants it known that anyone who starts or repeats such a dastardly rumor is going to have to deal with him... that he will defend Lorenzo against such preposterous charges."

"Jesus!" Martin exclaimed. "What is that going to accomplish?"

"It will get people talking."

"Yes... yes, I see," the elder Mazzavini nodded.

"You can start the leak by laughing at the absurdity of the rumor that Lorenzo has hand-written documents that say Greco tortured Paolo. Which, although you think they're ludicrous rumors, people will think explains why Giovanni gave his estate to Paolo's family. Giovanni never explained his reason for changing his will... but then neither did Antonio."

Massimiliano grew serious. "Do you know how long it would take for that misinformation to get back to Lorenzo?"

"I'm hoping it's in the half hour range," Beryl replied. "I do have other work waiting for me back in my office.

"Martin, here, can forge the documents once he sees the style of writing. As soon as she's out of the way, you'll start the rumor that there is a vicious story going around that you insist be squelched as soon as possible since you will not have the Calvino name sullied. It is preposterous to think that Alonzo Ruggieri sent 'memoir letters' to his wife in which he names Lorenzo and his wife as being torturers of Paolo. I can bring one of my partners back here and the three of us, Martin, my partner, and I will wait to see who breaks in to steal the letters. If you don't bring your 'would-be' killer out in the open now, you will never be free of him and neither will Martin or Ronald. You owe something to Ronald Calvino. This is your chance to make amends."

"It makes sense. They will want to get the proof against them," Martin said. "I'm in."

Beryl looked at Massimiliano who still had an expression of doubt. "Think about it. Lorenzo's worthless kids are scrambling to find new suckers to keep them in the style to which, etcetera, etcetera. They need to be marriageable. They don't want any of that old Mafia slime to cling to them. Contesting Giovanni's will is such a long shot... and now they'll know that there's more out there by way of proof against them than just your testimony. There are written documents. They will want them."

"Pop Pop," Martin said. "Beryl and I will go as soon as possible to get the papers from Mrs. Ruggieri and get her ready for a nice trip to Italy. Keep your new bodyguard nearby. Dress him up and take him into the clubs with you. You can say that he's a research assistant for Beryl's biography."

"Have you seen the fellow?" Massimiliano asked.

"No," Martin answered.

"He was a Canadian Football League linebacker. You do need to get out of the house more."

Beryl and Martin, carrying more Italian pastry, knocked on Maria Ruggieri's door expecting to find the thin old lady sick to her stomach from having eaten so many sweets. But instead she answered the door and her eyes lit up as she saw the boxes of pastries.

At the kitchen table she made strong tea, thanked Martin for paying the grocer, and scarfed down a cannoli.

Finally, she asked what she could do for Massimiliano's grandson.

"First," Martin said, "you could make it official by giving me a dollar as my fee to represent you just in case there is ever any problem in the future. I want you to be protected."

A strange sad look came over her face. "I don't got a dollar," she said. I'm waitin' for a check. I guess the holiday mail held it up."

"Do you have a dime?"

"Yeah... I have a dime." She went to the drainboard of the kitchen sink and found some change in a cup. "Here's a dime."

"I will accept this sum as a retainer for my services. Miss Tilson, here, bears witness to the agreement between us."

Beryl nodded and then smiled. "What case has she retained you for, Counselor?"

"The distribution of her husband's memoirs. Now, Mrs. Ruggieri," he continued, "I'd like to buy a few of Mr. Ruggieri's letters from you. And in exchange I'd like my friend here to take you downtown and get you... what do you call it?" he looked at Beryl.

"A makeover. New hairdo... some color... some makeup... a new wardrobe."

"And what I'm gonna do with that?"

"Go to Italy... courtesy of my grandfather."

"He's gonna come with me?"

"*Mrs. Ruggieri!* My Nana would not like that. She's jealous of pretty gals like you."

She laughed. "You can't blame a girl for tryin'," she said, "or dreamin'. My God! He was handsome." She got up and brought the box of letters to the table. "You see to it I get these back. Ok?"

"Of course. Is your birth certificate handy? We have to get you a passport."

"I've never had a passport. Italy! Can I go to Rome and Firenza?"

"Yes and Venice, too. And Naples. Tonight you can study a map of Italy and lay out the trip you want to take. Maybe a travel agency would help you. We'll go now and start your passport application. Just get your birth certificate. Beryl can pretty you up a little for your passport photo."

"When we gonna go downtown?" Marie Ruggieri went to the China cabinet in the dining room and rummaged through a pile of documents.

Beryl answered. "Martin's secretary will make the appointments for your hair. But we can get you the clothing tomorrow... and some new suitcases... shoes... bags... undergarments. Aside from the wardrobe and the free trip to Italy for a few weeks, ask me no questions and I'll tell you no lies. We girls do know how to keep a secret. I'll even see to it that you have a nice little camera so that wherever you go you can have someone take your picture."

THURSDAY, JANUARY 12, 2012

The three faked letters, according to Massimiliano, looked exactly like the originals once they had been folded, sat upon, and otherwise abused. Martin had found the handwriting easy to copy. It was much like the style he used to take notes at school. On the front of the page, he used the same sentimental phrases as he found in the other letters, and on the back of the page, he recounted the story of the abduction by putting together the accounts that Lucille, Parini, and his grandfather had given. He had the documents photocopied at the bank and certified as true copies. He would never testify that they were other than copies of his own creations. It was Lorenzo he needed to trick, not the court.

Martin called George and asked if he could come as backup for the weekend. "You needn't worry about traveling with a weapon. Months ago I bought a Cheetah which Beryl said you liked and a Colt Mustang which she said was a good second weapon. I can't really hit what I'm aiming at with either of them. Or with any alternative weapon. The gunsmith had me try a few of them. I need practice, he said. But the guns are here and you can use whichever one you want. She will be using my grandfather's Smith and Wesson. I don't know what caliber it is."

"What the hell are you talking about?" George said. "I thought you were supposed to be waiting inside some dilapidated house watching over old letters to see who would try to steal them."

"We are," said Martin. "But we don't know how many people will come in."

"Have concealed cameras placed around the goddamned place, inside and out, if you just want to see who comes for the letters. Three armed people hiding in a living room is a sure way for them to shoot each other.

And if they kill somebody else after baiting a trap, it's an ambush. And it isn't even your own house you're protecting. Where the hell is Beryl? Have you talked this over with her?"

"No. She's out shopping for clothing."

"That's just great. You're planning a massacre and she's out shopping. I'm going to get the next flight to Chicago. I'll let you know my e.t.a. and my carrier. You pick me up at the airport. I'll wear an Eagles jacket and a turtleneck sweater. I'll be there this afternoon. I'll call you right back." George hung up and called the airline.

Maria Ruggieri and Beryl went to the Mall and in a medium priced department store selected a suitable wardrobe for a widow to wear while traveling through Italy for several weeks in January. By lunchtime, she had purchased everything she needed, including a rolling suitcase. She left Beryl to keep her one o'clock appointment with the hairdresser that Martin's secretary had made.

The expedited passport was to arrive by Friday afternoon. Counting on the government's punctuality, Beryl would see to it that Maria was packed and properly attired and then she would accompany her to the post office to receive the passport. Since she was staying less than ninety days, she required no visa.

They would have a nice "going away" dinner and Beryl would take her to the airport. Martin had made her reservation on a late afternoon flight direct to Leonardo Da Vinci airport in Rome. The airline had suggested that she arrive two hours early and Martin suggested that three hours would be better.

Beryl asked for a favor, explaining that it was necessary for her own personal "assignment" that she be allowed to occupy the Ruggieri household during the weekend. Maria agreed as she primped in front of the mirror. "In my kitchen drawer, where I keep the silverware, are keys to the front door and the back door. You take them both. You like this color red? Or is it better to wear the blue?"

"Oh, the blue... definitely. It flatters your complexion."

By nightfall, George, Beryl, Martin and Massimiliano sat in Martin's apartment planning the events for Friday. All the weapons were on the coffee table. "I'm going to take a shower and go to bed," Beryl announced as she picked up her Beretta Tomcat. "Look at all that hardware, " she said. "Don't shoot each other. Remember, Boys! Make sure there's nothing in the chamber before you go pointing a gun. Play nice."

"Nobody likes her very much," Martin said.

FRIDAY, JANUARY 13, 2012

Massimiliano had brunch at several clubs and then, at two others, had lunch and a few drinks at the bar. He did not initiate any discussion about the Calvino family, but with masterful subtlety he managed to have his companions inquire about them. He naturally couldn't restrain himself from protesting vehemently the vicious rumors that were being circulated about Lorenzo Calvino. He asserted that he would happily support Lorenzo in any capacity. Not until he was sufficiently baited to reveal the wretched rumors, did he disclose Alonzo Ruggieri's hand written memoirs. He also spoke of Maria Ruggieri's foolishness in keeping her husband's letters at home. "The silly woman lives alone with dynamite like that in her cupboard."

Ronald Calvino asked himself what kind of CEO would he be if he didn't determine for himself who it was who was bugging his office. He had made a friend of the clerk in the electronics' store, he thought, when he purchased the recorder. In the few minutes he was inside the store he had asked, "If you wanted to secretly video your office to see who comes and goes in it, who would you contact to do the job?" The clerk gave him a business card and told him to be sure to mention his name since he would get a commission for the referral.

Calvino called the "surveillance man" listed on the card and on Thursday night, two cameras were secreted in his office, one in the bathroom - pointed discreetly at the dispenser - and the other on a shelf in his office - pointed at his desk. Additionally, two voice recorders were planted, one in the bathroom and the other near the doorway of his office. Experience had taught him that relatives and friends were the most likely individuals to jump a mining claim or to offer phony documents to support claims of mine ownership. He therefore had a device installed that would record both Dean Calvino's desk land line and his "on premises" cellphone calls.

While he admired Beryl and Martin's tenacity in locating his father's grave and solving the puzzle of the poem, he did not share their determination to protect Massimiliano Mazzavini. It had taken, he thought, a group of conspirators, men of differing abilities and social backgrounds, to effect the destruction of his father's life and the theft of his assets. At fourteen, he had been old enough not only to see his mother's suffering but to assume his father's responsibility to support his mother and sister. And while the conspirators reveled in their easy wealth, studying in landscaped schools, enjoying the camaraderie of fraternity houses, with weekends on skis or under sails, he knew the drudgery of walking to college night classes and dismal weekends that promised at best, time-and-a-half pay. He decided that he did not hate these people. He regarded them as vultures, creatures that were no doubt beautiful to each other but, even to the human onlooker who understood the task that nature had assigned them, they were still repugnant.

He had not realized how deeply he resented the lot of them until he attended Mazzavini's birthday party. He could never imagine the callousness the Calvinos had shown his mother when she was a pregnant teenaged girl, just as he could not now imagine what good they were doing that could possibly balance their cruelty to her. Certainly, giving her the ability to spend the last years of her life in an expensive home for the elderly was in no way compensatory. He remembered well the look of hopeless pain on his father's face when Antonio's will was read. And it was Massimiliano Mazzavini who had drawn up that will and no doubt knew the details of his father's exclusion. That the Lorenzo Calvino clan should be there, invited to celebrate Mazzavini's birthday with other honored guests, spoke to him more loudly and clearly than any proclamation of atonement and regret.

Ronald Calvino reasoned with himself, settling any doubts in his mind. His only aim was to learn who in his organization was spying upon him - and to what end. Naturally, he wanted to know who had harmed his father those forty years before; and, he determined, he would learn that sooner than later. To whatever extent Massimiliano Mazzavini had aided his grandfather in persecuting his father, he had, by his complicity, forfeited Ronald Calvino's concern. The old man's life was of little or no consequence to him. Had he known the full extent of Paolo Calvino's suffering, he would have been even more militant in his aims.

He did not know the specifics of the plan that Martin, Beryl, and George had formed to apprehend the person who came to the Ruggieri house to steal the letters. All he knew was that some kind of trap had been set that would occupy them, in shifts if necessary, throughout the weekend. Massimiliano Mazzavini would be at home with his wife and bodyguard. He decided that he would announce to his staff that he'd be having a long celebratory dinner with his family. But then, while he dined with his mother and son, he would excuse himself and say that he had to leave early to finish some work. His staff would see to it that the news that he would not be in his office would spread throughout the company.

He called his mother and son and asked them to join him for dinner. They agreed and Ronald Calvino asked his secretary to make reservations at a particularly fine restaurant downtown. She would have to select one, he said, since he did not know "the best watering holes" in Chicago.

Beryl escorted Maria Ruggieri to O'Hare airport. "It's a Friday night," she explained, "and Martin is right... you must be checked in well in advance of the flight. By morning you will be landing in Rome. Think of it!" Maria had a round trip ticket in business class. She would be comfortable during the ten-hour trip.

Beryl drove back to the Ruggieri house and parked her rented car two blocks away. She calmly went to the front door, unlocked it, and let herself in. Martin and George were already there. George had set up cameras that were concealed inside a teddy bear and a mantlepiece clock. The house had no fireplace and the Ruggieris had no children at home; but it was the best George could do on such short notice. He put the teddy bear on the couch and the clock on the sideboard, directly across from the china cabinet in which they had put the box of letters. They waited. Fortunately, Maria Ruggieri had not eaten all the pastry Martin had brought and George was able to retrieve some from the refrigerator's small freezer before Beryl, his official diet watcher, arrived.

Ronald Calvino and his family sat and marveled over the poem that had eluded them for so many years. "That's the problem with education today," Ronald Junior said, "everything is so incredibly specialized that no one gets a general education. e.e. cummings ought to be familiar to all of us. I saw a reference to one of his poems in a Woody Allen movie. Aside from that I'm totally ignorant."

"I remember that line from the movie," Lucille said. "When I saw it I remembered how your father used to quote it to me. 'Nobody, not even the rain, has such small hands.'"

Ronald also remembered his father quoting it. "It would have been a tip off, if we had only followed up and read the man."

"Dad," Ron Jr. said, "the point of being specialized is in being specialized. Who the hell had time to read poetry? When you want a business degree, you read the Wall Street Journal and Forbes."

The dinner was otherwise enjoyable and at 8:30 p.m. the check was paid by the breezy signature of the man who now held the reins of Calvino Investments.

Ronald returned to his office to see what the cameras had revealed. It did not occur to him that he might intercept the person who was trying to retrieve the tape in the bathroom towel dispenser.

At nine thirty, the elevator doors opened and he stepped out onto his office's floor. The cleaning people had already been through and only dim lights guided him as he walked down the corridor to his office. He could see his secretary's desk as he approached, and then as he turned toward his office, he saw that the door was open. He continued on, walking softly to the door. Inside, he could hear two voices, one male and one female. "We need new tape," the male voice said. "The recorder's coming loose."

The female voice replied, "I don't trust duct tape. Maybe his secretary has packing tape in her desk."

Ronald pushed the door open and confronted Dean Calvino and his mother Monica. He did not know what to say, or what to expect the intruders to say. He had gone to the trouble of installing equipment that would determine the identity of the person who was recording his phone calls, and he had returned to his office specifically to learn that identity. But as if he had expected only to encounter the person on film and not face-to-face, he stood there confused and speechless.

Monica Calvino was the first to speak. "He's alone," she hissed at her youngest son, "you can take him."

"Momma, for God's sake," Dean said resignedly, "take him where? We've been caught red-handed. It's over. This idiotic scheme of yours has just cost me my job and probably my career."

"No," she replied in a lilting voice, "we weren't caught red-handed. This *zoticone* invited us here. He told us he found out about his poor father's death. And when we got here he told us that he intended to kill us just to make the lie he told Giovanni seem like the truth." She picked up her purse and opened it, removing a weapon. "He tried to kill us with *this*! It's perfect! Oh, we'll tell the police how Ronald Calvino laughed at us and told us how he had lied to Giovanni. Yes, it was Ronald Calvino who told your uncle Giovanni that my blessed father, Salvatore Greco, and your father had tortured his father and castrated him with electric cattle prods!"

Ronald Calvino's face contorted into a look of horror. "Tortured" and "castrated" were words he had not even considered. He stood there transfixed, recalling how his father would not swim with him or let him in the bathroom when he was in the shower. These oddities had merely been scratches on his memory - they were not lacerations which, he now realized, they would have been if he had known the truth.

"So," Monica continued, misreading Ronald's expression and gesticulating with the gun, "you know we've got you. We'll simply say that you told Giovanni that Lorenzo and my father had tortured your daddy all those years ago. Tonight we'll be in possession of any letters that would have proven that. But you fabricated other evidence which you used to convince Giovanni to exclude Lorenzo from his will. Maybe you asked him, 'Do you want to leave your money to Lorenzo and the daughter of the man who tortured your baby brother?' Giovanni would have been so shocked. Yes, this is perfect! Perfect! And you were easily able to prove your lies to Giovanni. Didn't he send people down to Mexico? You got letters from one of my father's men. Ask the warden. Didn't Massimiliano's private investigators interview some of the old timers just recently? Sure. And isn't Maria Ruggieri on her way to Italy right now... new wardrobe and everything, courtesy of you? So you didn't want us to spoil your plan by revealing the truth... and that's why you fought with me and got this gun out of my purse... it saved you from having to use your own gun. Yes... you tried to kill us, but you didn't reckon on Salvatore Greco's daughter. I'm such a wildcat! Everybody knows that." She turned to Dino. "Isn't that how it went tonight?"

Ronaldo Calvino continued to stare at her. He was still fixed upon her words "tortured" and "castrated." He had made no attempt to follow the byzantine plot the elderly woman was outlining. He had seen Monica Greco Calvino in her insane response to the reading of Giovanni's will. She was crazy, he thought. Yes, he knew that there was a rumor that said he wanted to kill Massimiliano Mazzavini because the old attorney could expose the lie that he, Ronald, had supposedly told Giovanni Calvino. But beyond that, none of the story made any sense to him at all.

"So you see" Monica concluded her pitch to Dino, "he invited us to come here for a friendly talk. But what he really intended was to kill us to prevent us from telling the truth about him. I'm going to look after you, Dino. You should be the captain of this ship. This should be your office. Am I right? Huh! Am I right?" She pointed the gun at Ronald Calvino.

"For God's sake, Momma! Put that gun away! Nobody's gonna get killed over this. Why the hell did I ever listen to you? You've done enough damage to this family. Now, put the gun down!" He made a move towards her. Monica glanced sideways at him and fired the gun, missing Ronald by several meters.

Ronald Calvino stood like a statue still ossified by words that had revealed the truth of what to him had been ancient mysteries. Dino jumped at his mother and tore the gun from her hand. "Enough!" he shouted, handing the gun to Ronald who looked at it and placed it high on a bookshelf. He could hear a commotion near the elevators. Evidently the shot had summoned one of the security guards.

Dino had placed his mother in a side chair and, taking off his own jacket, he tied the sleeves around her and the back of the chair. He also took his belt off and anchored her abdomen to the chair as though it were a seat belt. She did not try to resist. The fantasy she had created was gaining credence in her mind. She began to speak as if she were telling her story to the police. "My husband Lorenzo eventually learned the truth about the Nievo family and what they did to Paolo; but he didn't want to talk about it and put my life and my father's life in jeopardy. He is such a thoughtful man. He could have squashed all those rumors at any time. But he loves us so much. He didn't want any trouble. Who knew why Antonio disinherited Paolo? Who knew what it was that Antonio believed? So when Ronald went to Giovanni and told him how my father tortured Paolo and blamed the whole airport financial fiasco on Paolo, Giovanni believed it and disinherited Lorenzo and me.

"And then my son, Dean, wrestled the gun away from him, and Ronald was accidentally shot!" She turned to her son and spoke in a weird conspirator's voice. "That will have to be at close range. Make sure you hit him in the heart or between his eyes. Make sure you kill him with the first shot."

A security guard had passed the secretary's desk and was advancing slowly toward Ronald's office. He appeared in the doorway with his gun drawn just as Monica began to realize that she was tied to a chair. She began to scream at Dino, calling him the most ungrateful, worthless child she had. She began to kick and flail her arms as the jacket began to loosen. "Do you have restraints?" Dean asked the guard, who immediately produced plastic zip ties and, with Ronald's help, secured her hands behind her.

"It's all right, Momma. We're gonna get you some help," Dino said. "We have to call a psychiatric ambulance for my mother. She's having a nervous breakdown. My cousin Ronald prevented a catastrophe from occurring. He could use a little treatment himself. He's evidently not used to guns."

"Where's the gun?" the security guard asked.

Dino reached for the weapon on the top shelf and handed it to the guard. As Monica continued to curse him, he pointed to the wall. "You'll find a slug from the gun in that wall. Thanks to Mr. Calvino's quick thinking, it missed me."

Monica Calvino was still screaming and cursing her son as the paramedics arrived. Dean assured everyone that he would see that Ronald got home safely. As he put his jacket on he said, "In the morning my cousin Ronald and I will both give statements to the police. Or you can contact our attorney, Martin Mazzavini."

Ronald finally spoke. "I'm very upset about this," he said to Dino and the guard. "I'm not likely to be coherent at this time. It's a sad thing to see someone descend into insanity. I'd like to get my bowels taken care of and then I'll sit at my desk for a few minutes. We can talk then." He went to the men's room and did nothing else except take the recorder from the towel dispenser. He put it in his pocket and returned to his desk. The guard stood up.

"Why don't you check the rest of the floor," Ronald suggested, and the guard left.

"Sit down," he said to Dean. "Let's hear what I missed." He played the tape and aside from his own conversations he heard only brief comments by Monica and Dean as they prepared to transfer the digital recording to another player. "The camera's not likely to reveal more. That bathroom camera, anyway."

"Are there more?" Dean asked.

"Yes," said Ronald. "The whole goddamned place has been bugged by professionals. Now tell me what you know about my father's death. What you know. When you learned it. And don't leave anything out."

Dean began slowly. "I came home early from summer camp one year... I must have been twelve... my mother and father were in the game room fighting. They fought a lot. My father shouted, 'You're the goddamned idiot who bid against herself!' I remember standing there listening. She yelled back, 'It was your friend in the Nievo family. My father should have killed you.'

"But that day that I came home early and listened I wondered what was my father doing with the Nievos? When they would start to fight, I'd pretend that I went out, but I'd sneak back in and listen and they would always talk about Paolo. My father delivered him to the Nievos and I guess we both know what happened to him."

"And my father went to Canada to get his genitals treated?"

"Yeah. I thought you knew. They removed his scrotum and put him on testosterone so he wouldn't get girly. He was one brave guy."

George had turned the porch light on as soon as he arrived at the Ruggieri house. It was still daylight then, but it was important that there be a light on for the sake of the camera and also so that no one would see a light being turned on when it grew dark. There also was a back door light, and he took the same precaution there. Now, sitting in the faint glow of the little nightlights that were plugged into several wall sockets, he, Beryl and Martin waited.

Maria had let everyone at the beauty parlor know that she was leaving for Italy that afternoon. "I'm gonna' see what everybody else saw. I'm gonna visit my mother's house and my Alonzo's house. Those houses are still in the family. Maybe I got cousins still living there. I'm gonna see for myself. And I wanna see those fountains everybody talks about. I make a wish. Three coins. I throw three coins in that fountain and make a wish. You don't wanna know what I wish for. Marone!"

Before she boarded her flight to Rome, everyone who had an interest in Alonzo Ruggieri's memoirs knew that she was gone.

At nine o'clock a shadow appeared through the tattered lace curtain of the front door's glass panel. Without a word, Beryl, George, and Martin

117

moved behind the couch and an overstuffed chair in the living room and, against George's better judgment, prepared their weapons to fire.

A second shadow appeared beside the first. Two men discussed "raking the tumblers."

In a moment the lock was sprung and the door opened. Lorenzo Calvino and his son, Tomas, entered the room and turned on a flashlight. The light circled the room.

"He said they're in the cupboard. That must mean the china closet," Lorenzo said in a normal voice. "That's where these old bags hide things."

Tomas opened the doors of the china closet as Lorenzo shone the light inside. "There's a lot of shit in here," Tomas said, "maybe they're in this box." He carried out the box and placed it on the dining room table.

George could see that Lorenzo had a gun in a shoulder holster. He mentally prepared himself for a violent struggle.

Tomas opened the box. "Here are a few that don't have envelopes - just a rubber band around them. They're beat up so they probably have been read more than the others. Let's see what we've got."

Lorenzo put his hand out. "You don't need to read them. Just hold the light."

Tomas took the flashlight and Lorenzo, turning slightly away, pulled one letter from the group, opened it and began to read. "Yes," he said, "this is one of them." He looked at the second letter and then the third. "These look like the whole episode. Let me read a couple of the others." He read one. "This is some job he pulled in Detroit. Bullshit. We've got the whole story. Let's get out of here."

As soon as they left the house and closed the front door, Martin said, "Call 9-1-1... a robbery's been committed here. I'm gonna make a citizen's arrest."

"Jesus!" George hissed and tried to stop him. But Martin was out the door just a few steps behind Lorenzo and Tomas. Beryl could do nothing constructive but turn her cellphone on and call emergency services.

"Hold it!" Martin yelled, pointing his Tomcat at the two men. "In accordance with chapter 725 of the Illinois Compiled Statutes I am hereby making a citizen's arrest. The police are on their way!"

Lorenzo's hand moved inside his jacket. George saw it and shouted, "So am I... a citizen... too. Get your hands up!"

Beryl, with her weapon drawn, also stepped down onto the sidewalk and removed Lorenzo's gun from its holster and put it in Martin's pocket.

The siren of a police car was heard in the distance and then the colored lights of the vehicle appeared at the end of the street. Beryl had already made Lorenzo and Tomas lean, spread eagled, against the car parked in front of the house. "I thought you were supposed to be writing a book!" Tomas snarled.

"Keep your mouth shut!" Lorenzo shouted.

Beryl's phone rang. Still holding the gun on Lorenzo, she answered. She listened and then said, "We had to leave our phones off. We were in a 'cone of silence' situation," she laughed and listened again and raised her eyebrows. "I'm delighted to hear it, Ron. Good work! I think we've hit a Grand Slam. Lorenzo and his son Tomas are in the process of being arrested, even as we speak." He could hear the sirens. "Yes," she said, "the police are here now. Listen! Can you bring your mother and have breakfast with us tomorrow? My partner George and I will be heading back to Philadelphia at noon."

Martin was looking at her waiting to hear the news. She asked him, "Where can we have breakfast with Ronald and Lucille? Monica and Dino are in custody. Ron caught them in his office. Monica tried to shoot him. She missed."

"Good news!" Martin shouted, poking Tomas. "The whole family can occupy a suite in Stateville. How about the club where we had my Pop Pop's birthday party?"

George, hearing Massimiliano Mazzavini called "Pop Pop" turned and looked at Beryl, and shook his head. As the police car pulled into a space several houses down from them, George took the gun Beryl was using and put it, along with the one he had been holding, into Martin's pocket.

Beryl continued to point her finger into Lorenzo's back. The police officers came up. "You got a permit to carry that weapon?" one asked Martin.

"Yes, I do. I'm Martin Mazzavini. I'm an attorney, an officer of the court. These men have just robbed the home of my client, Maria Ruggieri. The stolen items are in that one's pocket." He pointed at Lorenzo. "This is no simple B&E. They've also been trying to kill my grandfather, Attorney Massimiliano Mazzavini. So we'll be adding attempted murder charges."

"You'll all have to come down to the station," the other cop said, calling for backup and some advice from his captain.

SATURDAY, JANUARY 14, 2012

During breakfast, Martin made a point of explaining why his grandfather had no choice but to invite Lorenzo to the party. Ronald, grateful for the explanation, asked Martin to convey his apologies to his grandfather.

"I think the real reason they were invited," Martin guessed, "was that we needed some comic relief! They are a fun bunch."

Everyone laughed. Ronald wondered if the greatest punishment his cousins faced would be those striped prison suits. The laughter continued. It was an altogether pleasant occasion.

But it was time to go.

"Can't you leave her here?" Martin asked George as he loaded Beryl's suitcase into his car.

"No," said George. "We've given our statements to the police. Your grandfather's life is no longer in danger. And nobody's watching the store back home. She's been here almost two weeks. You won't be able to afford our bill as it is."

"How am I gonna get along without my Private Nag?"

Beryl cooed a response. "You can consult the *I Ching*. Or pick up a bloody phone! You can even come to Philadelphia," she said, mussing his hair. "You have friends there."

"When you least expect it, I'll be there. Will I have to sleep on the floor?"

George looked at him. "If I'm in her son's bed and she's in hers, you sure as hell will."

Beryl laughed. "Say goodbye to the handsomest Mazzavini for me," she said. "Tell him I look forward to waltzing with him again. And be sure to deliver Italian pastries regularly to the woman who, if the truth be told, is the one who solved the case for you."

"Truth? Did you say 'truth'?" Martin looked at Beryl, who grinned, knowing what was coming. "*You can't handle the truth!*" he said.

"*Son, we live in a world that has walls–*" Beryl's response was cut off as she found herself being shoved into the passenger's seat.

George slammed the car door shut. "The two of them should be put in quarantine."